Bargaining with the Boss

by
Catherine George

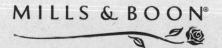

MILLS & BOON®

*MILLS & BOON and MILLS & BOON with the Rose Device
are registered trademarks of the publisher.*

*First published in Great Britain in 1997. This edition 2003.
Harlequin Mills & Boon Limited,
Eton House, 18-24 Paradise Road, Richmond, Surrey, TW9 1SR*

© Catherine George 1997

ISBN 0 263 83696 7

144-0404

*Printed and bound in Spain
by Litografia Rosés S.A., Barcelona*

PENNINGTON

A CHARMING COUNTRY TOWN –
BUT WHAT SECRETS LIE BENEATH?

Imagine...

A picturesque spa town and pretty villages that
nestle deep in the heart of England.

Pennington Country...

In Pennington the streets are filled with old-
fashioned buildings, attractive tearooms and
irresistible shops. In the surrounding villages of
Chastlecombe, Stavely and Swancote elegant manor
houses rub shoulders with cosy stone cottages, and
all the gardens are ablaze with flowers.

Pennington Lives...

And beneath the smooth surface the passions run
high – overwhelming attraction, jealousy, desire,
anger...and once-in-a-lifetime love.

Next month in Catherine George's
Pennington series:
THE PERFECT SOLUTION

Catherine George was born in Wales, and early on developed a passion for reading which eventually fuelled her compulsion to write. Marriage to an engineer led to nine years in Brazil, but on his later travels the education of her son and daughter kept her in the UK. And instead of constant reading to pass her lonely evenings she began to write the first of her romantic novels. When not writing and reading she loves to cook, listen to opera, browse in antique shops and walk the Labrador.

She has written over 60 romantic novels.

Praise for Catherine George:

'Catherine George...keeps readers thoroughly entranced.'
—*Romantic Times*

'Ms George has a captivating way of leaving her readers wanting more.'
—*www.theromancereadersconnection.com*

Dear Reader

Following (humbly) the example of Thomas Hardy and his Casterbridge, I decided to create my own fictional town for the location of many of my novels. The result is the Cotswolds town of Pennington Spa, a place of thriving modern commerce located in classical buildings which, like its Pump Rooms, date from the Regency era, when drinking the waters was all the rage. Having lived in two attractive county towns in the past, I've taken features from both and added fictional ones of my own to invent a town of wide streets, leafy squares and crescents, with buildings in the local golden stone and public gardens bright with seasonal flowers. There are several hotels, numerous restaurants, parks, cinemas, a theatre and, of course, irresistible specialist shops which sell clothes, jewellery, contemporary furniture and fine art, alongside others which offer bargains to the antiques hunter.

To me, Pennington and its nearby towns and villages – Chastlecombe, Swancote, Stavely, Abbots Munden – are the dream combination of prosperity and timeless charm. I just wish Pennington really existed, so I could live there.

Best wishes

Catherine George

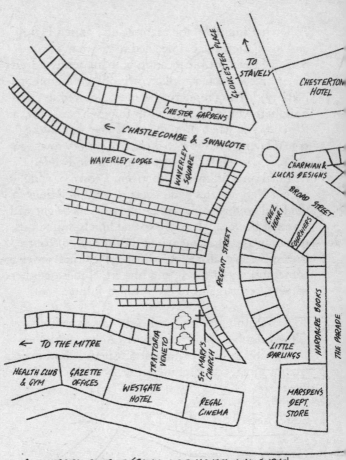

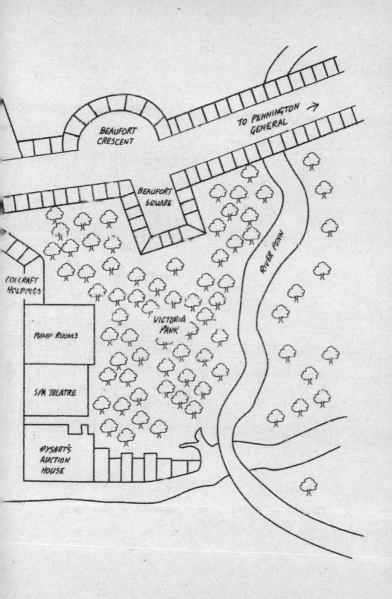

CHAPTER ONE

A BITING east wind blew flurries of snow across rolling uplands where Northwold Breweries blended with such ecological care into its Gloucestershire surroundings. The various specialist buildings and linking walkways were masked by skilfully landscaped banks and trees, and normally the sixty-acre site was a green and pleasant place. But on this particular January morning the stark white view from the managing director's office resembled a lunar landscape.

Eleri Conti arrived early, as she always did, and went into James Kincaid's office with her usual glow of anticipation for this first, private part of the day alone with him.

He was standing at the window, tall, loose-limbed, dressed in one of his dark custom-made suits and a flamboyant tie as usual. But when he turned his face wore a grim, haggard look so dauntingly different from usual that Eleri's smile of greeting died a sudden death. In her favourite black gabardine suit and white shirt, her dark hair caught back with a large ebony clasp, she faced him across the desk as she'd faced him at this hour almost every working day for the past year. But today something was obviously wrong.

The atmosphere was bleak enough to rival the day outside.

'Good morning, Eleri. I think you'd better sit down.' He waved her to a chair.

'Good morning, Mr. Kincaid.'

He sat staring down at his desk in brooding silence while Eleri grew colder by the second as all kinds of worrying scenarios crowded her mind, not least the loss of her job as personal assistant to the managing director.

At last James Kincaid squared his formidable shoulders and looked up, his eyes sombre. 'There's no way to make this easier. I wish there was. In short, Eleri, I've been informed that someone at this branch of Northwold leaked information about the Merlin takeover. As a result someone else made a nice little killing on the market.'

Eleri went white. 'And you are accusing *me* of leaking the information?' she asked in utter disbelief.

'No!' James Kincaid shook his head vehemently, raking a hand through his hair. 'Or at least not accusing. I'm merely asking if you know anything about it.'

'Which is the same thing.' Eleri had to exert rigid self-control to remain erect in her chair. She felt physically sick, as though the man opposite had dealt her a body-blow. Which, by doubting her integrity, he had. And worst of all she felt searingly hurt— because the accusation had been made by James Kincaid, for whom she cherished feelings kept strictly hidden. No one, either in Northwold or in her family, had the least idea that she was the victim of that tired old cliché: the secretary in love with her boss.

What, she thought bitterly, did she find so attractive about the man? He was far from classically handsome, with swarthy skin, unruly brown hair, forceful nose and a wide though well-cut mouth. Straight, dark brows above deep-set pewter-grey eyes warned the onlooker that this was no man to suffer fools gladly, and he wore his expensive clothes carelessly, as though from the moment he put them on he never gave them another thought. But, in comparison with James Kincaid, for Eleri all other men suffered. Willpower kept her utterly still in her seat as James took up a pen, rolling it between his fingers. Familiar with every little mannerism of his by heart, it gave Eleri deep satisfaction to see that he was affected— if only a little –by stress.

At last he looked up and began to explain rapidly. 'Eleri, just before the takeover went public on Tuesday, a trader in a London bank did a swift, profitable bit of dealing—buying Northwold shares at the old price then selling them a short time later when they rose quite sharply once the news was out. It was a relatively modest sum, and the trade only attracted attention because my sister's husband works for the same merchant bank. Up to that point the takeover was top secret.' He paused, his reluctance apparent as he added, 'Of the office staff here, you alone knew about this beforehand. And I know that a friend of yours works at the bank in question.'

Eleri stared at him in bitter disbelief. 'You really believe I would pass information to someone in a position to make use of it?' Her eyes flashed coldly. 'My friend would never do such a thing—even if I had been stupid enough to be so—so—'

'Indiscreet?'

'Unprincipled,' she corrected stonily. 'I told no one about the takeover, Mr Kincaid. No one. And I deeply resent your suspicions.' She jumped to her feet, but he waved her back to her seat.

'Sit down, please.'

The outer door opened and Bruce Gordon, the technical director, came in like a whirlwind. 'James, I need—' He stopped suddenly as he looked from James Kincaid to Eleri. 'Sorry.'

'Give us a few minutes, Bruce,' said James tersely, and the other man nodded, backing out hurriedly.

Eleri sat in silence, making no attempt to disguise her hostility as James Kincaid went on with his explanation.

'My brother-in-law,' he said heavily, 'works at Renshaw's, in the City.'

Eleri stiffened. Renshaw's was a merchant bank. And her friend, Toby Maynard, worked there on the trading floor. To mask her dismay she took the war into the enemy's camp. 'Did you tell your brother-in-law about the takeover, Mr Kincaid?'

His eyes hardened. 'No, Eleri, I did not. Nor would

it have mattered if I had. Sam would never have acted on it unlawfully.'

Knowing indignant protestations were useless, Eleri searched in her memory for some chance remark she might have let fall to Toby. Suddenly her face cleared. The last time she'd seen Toby she hadn't even known about the takeover! Her personal involvement had been in the final stages only.

'Until last week,' she said crisply, 'I knew nothing about the takeover. As you know very well, since you were the one who informed me one night last week when we were working late together. I've spoken to no one at all on the subject. And particularly not to the— the acquaintance in question, because he was in Val d'Isere on a skiing holiday until yesterday. Until last night I hadn't spoken to him for three weeks. He rang me last night, as soon as he arrived back.'

'If you mean someone by the name of Maynard, I'm afraid you were misinformed. He arrived back several days ago.'

Eleri's eyes flashed coldly. 'You're wrong! Besides, how could you possibly know Toby's the one—?' She stopped, biting her lip.

'You've obviously worked that out for yourself,' said James wearily after a long, uncomfortable pause. 'Sam told me. Maynard works for him—though of course he has no idea Sam is related to me, and therefore connected with Northwold, which is more to the point.'

The silence in the office deepened, emphasised by

the usual morning sounds outside as the administration block filled up with people arriving to complain about the weather and get on with the business of the day. Eleri was deaf to it all. She sat rigid, her mind going round in circles.

At last she got to her feet, her face bleak below the smooth black hair. 'Would you excuse me for a few minutes, please, Mr Kincaid? I need to make a phone call.'

He rose, nodding. 'By all means. I suggest you drink some coffee and come back in half an hour. We'll discuss this further.'

Eleri closed the connecting door behind her and sat down at her desk, then picked up her phone, punched out the number of Renshaw's Bank in the City of London and asked for Toby Maynard. When told he wasn't available, Eleri asked for Victoria Mantle instead.

'Vicky, it's me. Is Toby in today?'

There was a pause before her friend's reply extinguished Eleri's last flicker of hope.

'Eleri,' said the other girl, sounding miserable, 'Toby's gone.'

'Gone? What do you mean? Gone where?'

'Gone as in sacked, told to clear his desk and scram. Sorry, love. Toby's been a total idiot.'

'I've only just heard he came back early from Val d'Isere.'

'Didn't you *know*?' Vicky swore colourfully. 'He's been back for days. Look, he's probably at home.

Ring him. Give him hell. I've got to go. See you tonight, love. Bye.'

Eleri waited for a moment, pulled herself together, then rang Toby's flat and listened, frustrated, to the recorded message. 'It's Eleri, Toby. See you later,' she said swiftly, then put the phone down and stared blankly at the pile of unopened mail in front of her, feeling as though her world were falling apart. At last, with sudden decision, she typed quickly on the keyboard of her computer, waited while the letter was printed, then signed it. She pressed the button on her intercom, asked James Kincaid if she might come in, then went through the communicating door and crossed the large, orderly office.

Without a word Eleri handed over the letter, and waited. James read the few terse lines of resignation then jumped to his feet, glaring at her.

'I flatly refuse to accept this.'

Her chin lifted. 'You must see that in the circumstances it's impossible for me to work here any longer.'

He made a swift gesture of negation. 'Just give me your word you had nothing to do with the leak and we'll forget all about it.'

Eleri stared at him, incensed. '"Forget all about it"?' she retorted, no longer caring what she said. 'You accuse me of being a party to insider trading, and then expect me to carry on as if nothing had happened? Always supposing,' she added bitingly, 'that I managed to convince you I was blameless, of course.'

He scowled impatiently. 'Don't talk rot, Eleri. I assume you've tried to contact your friend?'

'Yes.'

'And?'

'He no longer works for Renshaw's.'

'That was inevitable.' The grey eyes held hers relentlessly. 'You tell me you haven't spoken to him on the subject, so Maynard obviously got the information from someone else.'

'He doesn't know anyone else at Northwold,' she said unhappily.

'Then you must admit I had no choice. I was forced to ask you about it.'

'Of course. So in the circumstances, Mr Kincaid, I don't have a choice either. I shall leave immediately. One of the other girls will fill in for you until you can find a replacement.' She smiled coldly. 'After all, it would hardly do to keep me on in a position of confidentiality. I'd never thought about leaking information for profit until you gave me the idea. How could I trust myself in future?'

'Nonsense,' he snapped, and jumped to his feet. 'Listen to me, Eleri. Your word is good enough for me. If you say you had nothing to do with it I believe you. And I understand your reaction. It's only natural you're angry. But don't act on impulse. Take time to reconsider.'

For a moment Eleri was tempted. But anger and

bitter hurt stiffened her resolve. She shook her head. 'I'm afraid not. It's out of the question.'

James Kincaid moved swiftly around his desk and seized her hand. She recoiled, startled, and he dropped her hand as though it burnt him.

'I'm not into sexual harassment,' he assured her coldly.

Eleri flushed. 'Of course not. I'm—on edge.'

'I merely meant to assure you that any reference you require is yours for the asking, if you're adamant about resigning. But I strongly advise you to change your mind. Go off now for the weekend, think things over.'

'I intend to find out what actually happened, certainly, but I won't reconsider. Nor will I need a reference,' she added.

His eyes narrowed. 'Why not?'

'A job is ready and waiting for me any time I say the word. With people who will never doubt my integrity,' she added, with a cold little smile.

'Eleri, *I* don't doubt your integrity,' he said with emphasis. 'I regret this as much as you do.'

'I doubt that,' she said bitterly, and went from the room, closing the communicating door behind her.

Bruce Gordon beckoned her into his office.

'James told me what happened—in strict confidence, of course,' he said. 'Go to that boyfriend of yours, beat the truth out of him, then come back here and get on with the job, my dear.'

'I'll certainly do the first bit, but I won't come

back, Mr Gordon.' Eleri shrugged, her face set. 'Even if I prove beyond all doubt that I said nothing about the takeover I can't work here now. But thank you for the vote of confidence,' she added warmly as James Kincaid came in.

'Eleri, come into my office before you go, please.'

'Of course.'

Eleri packed up her belongings, tidied her desk, deposited the morning's mail with one of the other secretaries, then went in to James Kincaid, who was standing at the window again, looking out on the blizzard conditions outside.

'You've been here for four years, Eleri,' he said, turning to her. 'This is a hell of a way to leave.'

'Yes. It is,' she agreed.

'When my predecessor handed over the baton he said he had only one piece of advice to give me. "Make sure you hang on to Eleri. She's worth her weight in gold."' He smiled crookedly. 'Damn good thing he's not here at the moment.'

'Mr Reeder and I got on well together.'

'Does that mean you've found it harder to work with me?'

'No.' She looked away. 'I believed we had a good working relationship too, Mr Kincaid. Until today.'

'We did. We *do*. I flatly refuse to look on this as final. Find out what happened,' he ordered, 'then come back to work on Monday.'

Eleri almost gave in, then and there. She liked her job. And she cared for James Kincaid even more. But his suspicions had cut like a knife. Yet in one way she had cause to be grateful for them. They had pushed her into the resignation which was the only cure for terminal hankering after a man who thought of her solely as a piece of efficient office equipment. 'I won't do that, Mr Kincaid,' she said at last. 'The mere fact that an official explanation is necessary makes it impossible for me to stay.'

He shook his head irritably. 'The explanation is purely for me. I've told no one about this, other than Bruce Gordon, and I only told him because he was about to offer me physical violence for upsetting you.'

Eleri smiled wryly. 'He's known me a long time.'

'I've known you a fair time myself—long enough to find your involvement in anything shady hard to believe.' He eyed her moodily. 'If you hadn't mentioned a friend at Renshaw's it would never have crossed my mind.'

She looked at him blankly. 'But the friend I told you about is a girl—Victoria Mantle. We grew up together.'

He frowned. 'Then where the hell does Maynard come in to it?'

'Vicky introduced him to me a few months ago at a party.' She looked him in the eye. 'Toby's just a friend. I wasn't even aware you knew anything about him.'

'I didn't. My sister's husband, Sam Cartwright, told me Maynard confessed he got the information from someone at the brewery, but wouldn't disclose the name. I put two and two together—and got five,' he added, his jaw tightening.

'I can see why you thought it was me,' she said bleakly.

'You say it wasn't, so I believe you. Nevertheless, I was forced to ask for an explanation, Eleri.'

'I want one, too,' she said bitterly. 'I'm leaving right now for London to get it.'

'I can't tell you how much I regret all this, Eleri,' said James heavily. 'Do you really have another job waiting for you?'

'Oh, yes,' she said, resigned. 'I'll be welcomed with open arms.'

'And no reference needed.' He raised an eyebrow. 'I'm curious. You speak Italian, of course. Will the new job use your bilingual talents?'

'More or less.' The telephone interrupted them, and Eleri answered it automatically. 'Mr Kincaid's office.'

'Camilla Tennent,' said a light, feminine voice which had become all too familiar to Eleri over the past year. 'Is James there?'

Eleri handed the phone over. 'Miss Tennent,' she announced, and left the room to collect her belongings, feeling deeply depressed. James Kincaid was a clever, ambitious man, relatively young for the post he held, and with his sights very obviously set on a seat on the Northwold board. He'd been at the Gloucestershire brewery only a year, but already he'd streamlined the plant to an efficiency which surpassed the other Northwold operations. She would have liked to stay, to be part of James Kincaid's success story. But Toby Maynard had put paid to all that in the space of a few minutes' trading.

Before leaving, she rang her mother. 'I'm leaving for London early.'

'I thought perhaps you wouldn't go in this weather,' said the familiar lilting voice. 'Drive carefully to the station, *cariad* When are you coming back?'

'I'm not sure. I'll ring and let you know.'

'Don't forget. You know what your father's like.'

'Who better?' said Eleri dryly. 'Must dash. See you soon. Bye.'

Then she rang Vicky to give her appalled friend the news. Afterwards she took one last look round her office, said goodbye to her colleagues on her way out of the administration block, then left to drive to the station, thirsting to confront Toby Maynard. She kept mulling over his treachery in the train, cursing the day she'd ever laid eyes on him. Early in life, disaster had taught Eleri to keep to strictly platonic friendships with the relatively few men she knew. Toby was young, fun to be with, and had taken her out sometimes when she spent weekends at Vicky's London flat, but Eleri had always slept in Vicky's spare bed afterwards. Her relationship with Toby had been pleasant, but unimportant. Yet, unbelievably, it had cost her the job at Northwold.

When Eleri left the train in London she took a taxi,

hoping Toby would at least be able to provide her with some hot coffee. Wine was usually more available than milk in his smart Chelsea flat. Toby preferred to eat out. Even his breakfast cappuccino and toast had been, until recently, bought *en route* to Renshaw's to eat at his desk.

Toby was not at home. Eleri ground her teeth in frustration, and was halfway down the street on her way to the Underground, and Vicky's flat in Ealing, when Toby came loping into view, laden with grocery sacks. He looked tanned and casually elegant in a hooded ski-jacket and thick jogging pants tucked into costly leather boots. Normally he often looked haggard, like most young men in his profession, but his holiday had smoothed away the telltale signs of stress, and even dressed for a snowy day he looked immaculate—as always. He smiled in delight, and tried to kiss her cheek.

'Eleri, you're early—hey, what's the matter?'

She pushed him away, glaring. 'You've actually got the nerve to ask me what's the *matter*?'

He thrust flopping, expensively cut fair hair back from his face, looking sulky. 'Oh, hell. I suppose you rang me at the bank.'

'Yes, Toby, I did exactly that. You weren't there, so I spoke to Vicky—'

'And she gave you all the dirt, I suppose.' He unlocked his door, eyeing her morosely. 'She told you I got the push?'

'Of course she did. Not that it came as a surprise.'

He glared at her indignantly as he ushered her inside. 'Why not?'

Eleri controlled her temper with effort. 'Apply the little grey cells, Toby!'

He sighed. 'I suppose she told you about my little profit-making venture.'

'Actually, no, she didn't.'

'Really?' He shrugged. 'All I did was take a chance. I'd been unlucky lately, El, I needed to recoup.'

'Recoup?' Eleri stared at him stonily. 'What for, Toby? A Ferrari instead of your Chelsea Tractor?'

'You got that stupid name from Vicky, I suppose!' he snapped. 'It's a Range Rover, and I've no intention of getting rid of it.'

'So what did you want the money for? But never mind that. For starters, I heard you came back on Monday, not last night.' Her dark eyes speared his. 'It doesn't matter a toss to me when you came home, Toby. But why on earth lie about it?'

He reddened. 'I was going to tell you about it today. But—oh, blast, you assumed I'd just got back, so I left it. Why the fuss?'

She advanced on him like a tigress. 'Don't worry, Toby,' she bit out when he recoiled, 'I'm not going to hurt you, but I am going to make a "fuss", and you are going to listen.'

'Can I put this stuff away first?' he said, backing away in mock alarm.

'Yes, of course. And I hope you bought milk. I'm dying for some coffee.'

A few minutes later they were seated on opposite sides of the fireplace where Toby put a match to the logs for the blaze he liked—as much for image, Eleri suspected, as to keep warm.

'So carry on, Eleri,' he said with a sigh. 'Make your fuss. Though I could do without it at the moment.'

'Tell me what happened first.'

He eyed her mutinously, then shrugged. 'In a nutshell, I gambled and lost.'

'But gambling's your job.'

'My job, sweetheart, is to make money for Renshaw's. Only recently I began to lose it more than make it. I began to get panicky—bad news for a trader. Another significant loss, and I was in the mire.' He stared at the crackling flames. 'Then in Val d'Isere I met a girl.'

Eleri was unsurprised. Although Toby enjoyed himself more with a bunch of men-friends than with women, he liked girls as pretty accessories to take to parties—and to bed. But when Eleri, right from the first, made it plain bed was never an option where she was concerned, Toby, surprisingly, had accepted it without question.

'Go on,' she said quietly.

'Her name's Arabella Pryce—fabulous skier and great fun. She was actually a chalet girl at the place the gang was staying. Quite a coincidence, really, because I'd met her before when she was a kid—I was in school with her brother Julian. Anyway, Bella and I got on like a house on fire from the start, and—well, you know, one thing led to another—'

'Spare me the details, Toby,' said Eleri wearily, looking at her watch. 'And hurry it up. I'm catching a train soon.'

He stared at her in astonishment. 'But you've only just got here! Dammit, Eleri, surely you're not dumping me just because I had some fun on holiday?'

'No,' she said with perfect truth. 'But it's a contributory factor.'

'It didn't mean anything,' he said in consternation. 'I only brought Bella's name in to it to explain getting fired—'

'How did a holiday fling get you fired, for heaven's sake?'

'I'll tell you if you'll let me finish!' He shook his hair back. 'To cut a long story short, I boasted a bit about juggling with millions in my job, and Bella said what a shame I was on holiday, because she had a hot tip to give me. About the Merlin takeover the following Tuesday. Her family own Merlin Ales. Or did.'

'So you leapt from her bed and caught the next plane home!'

'I didn't do anything of the kind! I merely flew back on Monday instead of yesterday,' he said, injured. 'It seemed the perfect way to recoup my losses—I wasn't even out for personal profit.'

'How very high-minded of you. But aren't you leaving something out, Toby?' she asked.

He frowned. 'I don't think so.'

'It was Northwold who took Merlin over, not the other way round,' she said angrily. 'And just in case it slipped your mind, I work for Northwold. Or did until today. Your little escapade cost me my job.'

Toby stared at her in horror. '*What*? How the hell could it do that?'

'They think your inside information came from me.'

He swore colourfully and at some length. 'What can I say, darling? I never thought about you.'

'Which is glaringly obvious! You know someone called Sam Cartwright at Renshaw's, I believe?' she demanded.

'Damn right I do. He's the chief executive—the swine who told me to clear my desk,' said Toby bitterly.

'And although you gallantly shielded Miss Pryce by withholding her name, you did say the information came from the brewery. But you forgot to say which one.' Eleri glared at him in fury. 'Sam Cartwright happens to be the brother-in-law of James Kincaid— the man who was my boss until this morning. The boss who concluded *I* was your source!'

'The man fired you because of me?' Toby flung himself on his knees in front of her and caught her hands. 'Eleri, I'm so *sorry*.'

'He didn't fire me. I resigned.' Eleri freed herself

and sat up straight. 'Cut the drama, Toby. Penitence doesn't suit you.'

He jumped up and stood over her, the picture of misery. 'What a mess. I wish I'd never set eyes on Bella.'

'Toby, don't try to shift the blame.' Eleri eyed him with distaste. 'The lady was indiscreet, maybe, but you were the one who acted on the information.'

'Don't rub it in!'

'What will you do about a job now?'

'I've got contacts—in fact I'm seeing someone on Monday.' He grinned sheepishly. 'Old school chum.'

Eleri shook her head. 'Someone may strangle you with that old school tie of yours one day.'

'Is there anything at all I can do to put things right for you?' he said, sobering.

'No fear. You've done enough already.' She jumped to her feet. 'Right. Ring for a cab for me, please, Toby. If I leave in a few minutes I'll make the next train home.'

'What's the point of going home?' he demanded, looking so crestfallen she almost laughed. 'I thought you were staying with Vicky as usual. We could go out to dinner, then see that new Branagh film if you like, and tomorrow I'll get tickets for the theatre—'

'You do that, by all means. But not with me.' Eleri shrugged into her coat, then handed him his key. 'Our platonic little arrangement—pleasant and diverting though it was—is terminated as of today.'

'You don't mean that!'

'Oh, but I do.' She smiled up into his sulky, good-looking face. 'You're a clever lad in a lot of ways, Toby—Cambridge first in Maths included. But the key word there is "lad". You need to grow up a bit.'

He coloured angrily. 'I'm not *that* much younger than you!'

'Not in age, maybe. Otherwise you're still a baby,' she assured him acidly. 'By the way, Toby, isn't there something you should be asking *me*?'

He stiffened, eyeing her apprehensively. 'Er—what, exactly?'

Eleri laughed in his face. 'What *did* you think I meant? Wouldn't it be good manners to enquire about my own plans now I've lost my job?'

'Oh, hell—you make me feel like such a worm,' he muttered, reddening. 'But someone with your experience shouldn't find it hard to get another job.' His blue eyes widened. 'This Kincaid chap you work for wouldn't withhold a reference, would he?'

'I'm afraid he might,' she sighed, wanting him to fry a little. Her smile was as wistful as she could make it. 'But don't worry about me, Toby. I'll get by. Somehow.'

CHAPTER TWO

ELERI locked the door to the street, switched on the lights and the coffee-machine, then moved round the pretty, bright café to check the tables, making sure all the menus and condiments were in place. Satisfied all was ready for the next day, she pulled down the blinds and went back behind the counter. Next door in the restaurant she could hear the waiters talking as they performed similar tasks to hers, except for them work was only just beginning, and customers would soon come in to choose from a three-page menu of dishes from various regions of Italy, plus a list of British favourites to suit less adventurous tastes.

Eleri's domain was the coffee-shop, where customers came in from early morning onwards to drink capuccino and eat teacakes and pastries and the cinnamon toast which was Conti's speciality. At lunchtime the café served pizzas, or huge flat buns filled to order with salad and seafood or thin Italian ham, and in summer tables were set outside under umbrellas in the cobbled square in front of St Mark's church—like a small piece of Italy set down in the Englishness of the shire town of Pennington.

It was a mere two weeks since Eleri had resigned her job at Northwold to return to the fold, and already she felt as if she'd been back in the family business forever. Her father had come to Britain from Italy thirty years earlier to work in his uncle's restaurant, where he met Catrin Hughes, a black-haired Welsh beauty on the same catering course. As soon as they finished their training the pair got married, and with their combined skills formed an unbeatable team. They took over the running of the restaurant, re-vamped the menu and the decor, and rapidly attracted a much larger clientele. When Mario's uncle died he left the business to them both, whereupon the ambitious young Contis took over the premises next door to add the kind of coffee-shop the holidaying British public had learned to appreciate on trips to Italy and France.

In the first years of their marriage Mario and Catrin Conti were blessed with two daughters, Eleri and Claudia. Then, after a long interval, Niccolo Conti opened large blue eyes on the world and Mario Conti finally gained a male heir to his small, but profitable empire.

These days Mario left the actual cooking to four skilled chefs and confined himself to the financial side of the business, but he put in an appearance at the restaurant most nights. Until her marriage Claudia had run the coffee-shop, but Eleri, from the first, had never wanted to work in the family restaurant in any capacity. After gaining a degree in English, she fol-lowed it with a business course with her friend, Victoria Mantle, who made straight for a career in

London afterwards. But Eleri had always worked within travelling distance of Pennington and lived at home, her annual holidays and occasional weekends in London with Vicky her only breaks from her close-knit Italianate family background.

Now Claudia was married, and Eleri's resignation from her job had been greeted with passionate enthusiasm by her family. She'd decided to make the best of it and began to run the coffee-shop with the efficiency previously brought to her job at Northwold. Within days she'd taken over the ordering for the entire business, which prided itself on using the freshest of produce from local suppliers wherever possible. Each day she ordered meat, fish and vegetables from the local market and bread from a nearby bakery, while the ice-cream for which Conti's was renowned came from an Italian supplier based in the Welsh valleys.

At six o'clock, as she did every evening, Eleri locked up, popped her head round the door of the restaurant and had a chat with Marco, the head waiter, then took herself off to the family home tucked away in a quiet cul-de-sac behind the trattoria.

'You look tired,' said her mother, giving her a kiss. 'Finding it hard, *cariad*?'

'My feet find it hard, but the rest of it's easy enough.' Eleri sank into a kitchen chair, watching as her mother stirred sauce in a pan. 'The trouble is Mamma *mia*, that although I like dealing with the general public, especially the regulars, and I quite enjoy the ordering and haggling with the suppliers and so on—'

'You miss your work at Northwold.'

'Exactly.' Eleri smiled. 'Clever old thing.'

'Not so much of the old,' said her mother, then looked up with a smile as her husband came in. 'Good timing, Mario, your dinner's ready. Eat it now so you can digest it before you go over to the restaurant. Eleri, you can have a bath before you eat, if you like.'

'I do like, Ma. My feet are killing me.' Eleri yawned widely.

Mario Conti was an elegant, olive-skinned man with a head of thick, greying blond hair and heavy-lidded blue eyes. He kissed his wife lovingly, then turned to his daughter. 'So, *cara*. How was your day?'

'The same as usual. Quite busy, in fact. The takings were well up on yesterday.'

Mario Conti looked at his daughter's tired face, frowning. 'I was asking how *you* were, not the takings.'

'I'm fine,' said Eleri, heaving herself out of her chair. 'And I'll be even better after dunking my poor aching feet in a hot bath! Nico's at football practice, I assume?'

'Where else?' said Mario dryly.

Eleri laughed, and went upstairs, knowing perfectly well her parents would be deep in discussion over their elder daughter the moment she was through the door. In the bathroom she shared with Nico, Eleri let herself down into hot, scented water with a sigh of relief, grateful that her mother appreciated her need for time to herself. She loved her family, but, unlike Claudia, who'd been perfectly happy to live at home and work in the family business, Eleri had enough of her independent Welsh mother in her to need her own space from time to time. She missed her work at Northwold—and James—so badly that sometimes it was a struggle to disguise the fact from her parents, who knew nothing of her fight to forget James Kincaid. Eleri's sloe-black eyes kindled at the memory of his suspicions. Forget him she might. In time. But forgiving him was something else entirely.

At least she was lucky to get the bathroom to herself tonight, she thought with a grin. Nico wanted to be a football star, not a restaurateur. But whether he achieved his ambition or not the security of the trattoria would always be waiting for him. Just as the coffee-shop had lain inexorably in wait for herself.

Eleri sighed, got out of the bath, and pulled on jeans and thick yellow sweater. She dried her hair, anchored the front strands behind her ears, then thrust her throbbing feet into soft boots bought on a visit to her grandparents in the Veneto the previous spring. She stared into the mirror moodily. She was the odd one out in the family in more ways than one; the only one with the Welsh name Catrin had insisted on for her first child. Claudia had fair curling hair and blue eyes, like their father, but Eleri's straight black hair and wide-set dark eyes came from her Welsh mother. It was a family joke that Eleri looked more Italian than any of the family—even Nico, whose mane of wild black hair and brilliant blue eyes played havoc with the girls in school.

When Eleri was clearing up after her solitary, peaceful supper the phone rang.

'*Cara,*' said her father. 'Marco told me a man was asking for you in the restaurant earlier.'

'Who, Pop?'

'Like an idiot Marco forgot to ask—it is busy in there tonight.'

Eleri was curious as she put the phone down. Surely Toby hadn't been misguided enough to come looking for her at the trattoria? She'd been forced to tell her parents why she'd resigned from Northwold, and her father had needed much spirited argument from his womenfolk to prevent him rushing up to London to confront the young man he'd never approved of for his daughter, however casual the relationship. Not that Mario approved of any man for his daughters. Fortunately Claudia had married a solid, dependable young man with a steady job in an accounting firm. But secretly Eleri knew very well she was Mario's darling, partly because she was the one who argued with him most and stood up to him, but mainly because she was the image of her mother at the same age. And because of it he was harder on her than on his other children. A man would have to be something very special indeed before Mario Conti approved of him for his elder daughter.

Not, thought Eleri morosely, that her father had

need to worry on that score at the moment, if ever. After confronting Toby in London she'd refused to speak to him on the phone, and after the first few days he'd given up. Nowadays she worked a six-day week, which ruled out weekends in London with Vicky. She did her best to put on a good face, but sometimes she felt claustrophobic, even caged, and missed James Kincaid far more than she missed Toby. The day James arrived at the Gloucestershire plant of Northwold Eleri had taken one look at him and known that she would stay with him all her working life if he wanted her to. But in a few short minutes of trading Toby Maynard had put an end to her time at Northwold, and changed her life for ever.

The coffee-shop was very busy next day. Saturday always brought more shoppers into town and a gratifyingly large number of them came into Conti's for hot drinks to keep out the biting January cold. Just before midday, when Eleri was taking a few minutes in the little room at the back, glad of some coffee and a breather before the lunchtime rush resumed in earnest, one of her assistants popped round the door.

'Sorry to interrupt—a customer's asking for you.'

'Who is it, Luisa?' said Eleri, getting up. 'Anything wrong with her meal?'

'No.' The girl grinned. 'It's a him, not a her, and he hasn't had a meal yet. Gianni's just making a sandwich for him. I thought you might prefer to serve it to this particular customer—table ten.'

The table was against the window in the far corner

of the café, and seated at it, reading a newspaper, was James Kincaid. Eleri's heart turned a somersault under her dark red sweater, but her hand was steady as she set a beautifully garnished sandwich in front of him. He put the paper down and jumped to his feet, smiling in a way which did nothing to slow her heartbeat.

'Eleri—thank you. I hoped you'd spare me a minute. Won't you join me?'

She smiled politely. 'I'm afraid not. This is our busy time. Do sit down again.'

'I can't if you don't.'

Eleri cast a swift glance towards the counter, where her two assistants were trying to hide their curiosity while they worked. For the moment the café was only half full, and it was obvious they could cope.

'Mr Kincaid—' she began, seating herself.

'Now we're on your territory couldn't you make it James?' He bit into the sandwich with appreciation. 'Mmm, this is good. Where do you get the salmon?'

'From the market. We buy all our produce there.' She sat, composed, waiting for him to explain his presence. He looked very different in sweater and heavy tweed trousers, a waxed jacket slung over the back of his chair. The mere sight of him gave Eleri a sharp pang of longing for Northwold, her job—and James.

'How are you?' he asked.

'I'm fine,' she assured him, knowing she sounded

cold in her effort to hide her pleasure at the sight of him.

'It took some detective work to find out where you were. This, I take it, was the job waiting for you whenever you said the word?'

Eleri nodded. 'My parents were shocked by my resignation from Northwold, of course, but otherwise they were delighted to welcome the prodigal back to the fold.'

'Which brings me to my reason for coming here,' he said, leaning forward.

'Excuse me, Eleri,' interrupted a diffident voice. 'The bakery's on the phone.'

'Right, Gianni.' Eleri got up, smiling at James in rueful apology.

'Excuse me.'

The phone call was lengthy, involving confirmation of extra supplies for the wedding party they were catering for next day. By the time Eleri was free every table in the café was full, and James Kincaid was on his feet, dressed ready for the street as he handed her the bill and money for his lunch.

'I won't hold you up any longer,' he said as she gave him his change.

'Sorry. We're always busy on Saturdays.'

'I called in last night, but you'd already gone.' He paused. 'Do you work in the evenings?'

She shook her head. 'Only in emergencies—like tomorrow, when there's a wedding party. Otherwise I work an eight-hour day, six days a week.'

'No sinecure then—longer hours than Northwold,' he commented, and raised an eyebrow. 'Which brings me once more to the reason for my visit. I'd like a talk with you. It's short notice, I know, but would you have dinner with me tonight?'

Eleri stared at him in astonishment, and only managed to control instant, rapturous consent by turning away to deal with a customer waiting to pay for lunch. She made the transaction, exchanging a few pleasantries, glad of the respite to gather her wits together, very conscious of the tall man studying the family photographs on the wall in the little foyer between the coffee-shop and the restaurant. When she was free he turned back to her.

'I suppose it was too much to hope for on a Saturday night.'

That wasn't the point, she thought, knowing perfectly well she ought to refuse. She was doing her utmost to get over James Kincaid. A dinner date was hardly the way to go about it. 'It's very kind of you—' she began.

'Not in the least,' he interrupted. 'You'd be doing *me* a kindness if you would.'

Why? she wondered. Perhaps he was at a loose end because Camilla Tennent was skiing in Gstaad or sunning in the Bahamas or wherever. 'I'm afraid—'

'Don't say no,' he said swiftly. 'Look on it as a business appointment.'

Aware that Luisa and Gianni were in a frenzy, trying to cope with the lunchtime rush, Eleri gave in. To

James and herself. 'Oh, very well—' She broke off to smile at a customer. 'Just one moment, sir, I'll be with you directly.'

'What time shall I pick you up?' asked James, and handed her a banknote. 'Give this to your staff.'

'How kind, thank you. But don't come for me. I'll meet you somewhere.'

'The Mitre about eight?'

'Yes. Right. Now I really must go.' She turned away and plunged back into the business of heating pizzas and pouring coffees, and anything else necessary to relieve the beleaguered young pair who worked so willingly for her.

'You're going out?' said her mother in surprise when a very weary Eleri went home later that evening.

'Yes. Not that I feel like it. I'm done in.'

'They why go?'

'Curiosity, I suppose.'

Catrin Conti eyed her daughter warily. 'It's not with that Toby, I hope.'

'What would you do if I said yes?'

'Worry my head off.'

Eleri relented, giving her mother a hug. 'Don't, it's not Toby. Though you'll never guess who. I can't believe it myself. The person asking for me last night was James Kincaid.'

'Your boss at Northwold?' said her mother, astonished. 'Never!'

'He came to the coffee-shop lunchtime, but I was

too busy to talk to him much, so he asked me out for a meal tonight. Said it was business.' Eleri thrust her hands through her hair, then looked at her watch. 'Heavens, it's later than I thought—better get my skates on.'

'Business, is it! Where's he taking you?'

'The Mitre.'

Catrin sniffed. 'You'd eat better here.'

'Very possibly. But not with the same privacy, Mamma *mia*,' said her daughter mockingly. 'Where's Nico?'

'Gone to the pictures with the usual gang.' Catrin smiled. 'He's helping out with the wedding party tomorrow night, by the way, to earn extra pocket money.'

'New football boots, I suppose.' Eleri laughed and went upstairs for a bath, more excited than she cared to admit, even to herself, about the forthcoming evening with James Kincaid.

She took enormous care with her hair and face, then went downstairs to find her father still at home.

'Pops, my car sounds a bit funny. I think I'd better take a taxi.'

Her father's eagle eye took in her wool tunic and long, clinging skirt, the soft kid boots and heavy gold earrings.

'Lady in black—*bellissima*,' he said, eyes narrowed. 'All this for the man who fired you from Northwold?'

Ouch, thought Eleri. 'He didn't fire me. I resigned.

I'm curious to know what he wants, that's all. He said it was business.'

'A man takes out a woman who looks like you, he does not think only of business,' declared her father wryly. 'Not if he has blood in his veins.'

'Don't judge all men by yourself, Pa!' she said.

He laughed, and kissed her. 'I'll ask Luigi to look at the car in the morning.'

'Come on, Mario,' said Catrin. 'We're needed in the restaurant. Enjoy yourself, Eleri!' She kissed her daughter's smooth olive cheek. 'You look gorgeous, love.'

Eleri waved them off, knowing she looked her best. The tiredness of the day had vanished after her leisurely bath. She'd left her hair loose to skim her shoulders, added a touch more emphasis to her eyes than usual and, best tonic of all, she was spending the evening with James Kincaid. She grinned at her reflection in the hall mirror. 'You'll do, Conti. Ring for a taxi.'

When Eleri arrived at the Mitre James was waiting for her in the courtyard, and had paid off her driver before she had time to ask the fare.

'Eleri, hello,' he said, smiling, as they went inside the inn. 'Thank you for coming.'

'I said I would.'

'I thought you might have had second thoughts.'

'If I had I'd have rung to let you know,' she assured him.

James managed to secure a small table in a corner

of the crowded bar for a lengthy perusal of the menu over the drinks he ordered.

'I'm told the restaurant here is rather good, but with you it's a bit like taking coals to Newcastle. I hope it comes up to your standards,' he said, raising an eyebrow at her.

'As long as it's not pasta in any shape or form I don't mind,' she assured him, smiling. 'No one does pasta dishes like our chefs. Though my father's the master,' she added, 'when he's in the mood to cook.'

'Does your mother cook, too?'

'Brilliantly. But only at home. She cooks dinner about four times a week, and the other nights we fend for ourselves, or they send something over from the restaurant. Nico eats like a horse.'

'Nico?'

Eleri smiled, her eyes soft. 'He's fifteen, clever, and pretty gorgeous, actually.'

'And his big sister obviously dotes on him!'

She flushed. 'I suppose I do. Nico dreams of playing soccer for Inter Milan—though he might just deign to sign for a top English club if begged, of course.'

'Big of him!' James grinned. 'Though I can sympathise. I always wanted to play international rugby—wear the white shirt for England and all that.'

'Then you're the enemy! I cheer for the Welsh.'

His eyebrows rose. 'Really? Italy I could understand, but why Wales?'

'Because my mother's Welsh. Hence my name,' she explained.

His eyes gleamed ruefully. 'Is Eleri Welsh? I thought it was something obscurely Italian. I went on calling you Miss Conti at first because I wasn't sure I was pronouncing it properly.'

'I remember. You addressed all the other girls by their surnames, too!'

'I had to,' he confessed, 'once I started it with you.'

Eleri chuckled. 'How funny. We all thought you were too high and mighty to descend to first names with the hired help.'

'Did *you* think that?' he said, startled.

'Of course I did.'

'Your name was to blame.' He smiled wryly. 'I heard Bruce and the others using it, but I always thought they were wrong. It doesn't sound the way it's spelt.'

'To rhyme with fairy—or contrary, according to my father. We lock horns sometimes.'

'Would it be rude to ask why?'

'Not in the least. My protective Italian father likes to keep his girls close under his eye. But my mother supported my determination to go to college, because she did. And because my father would do anything in the world for her he agreed.' Eleri smiled into his intent face. 'But surely you didn't ask me here tonight to hear my life story?'

'It's fascinating. The combination of Celt and Latin sounds explosive!'

'It is, on occasion. But any disagreements are short-lived. My parents' relationship is a very special one.'

'It's the same with my parents. Both pairs are to be congratulated. Long-running successful marriages are thin on the ground these days.' James looked up as a waiter appeared to take their orders. 'Right then—Eleri. What would you like to eat?'

Realising that whatever the reason James Kincaid had for asking her here tonight she was unlikely to learn what it was until they'd eaten, she asked how things were at Northwold, a subject which lasted until they were called in to dinner in the adjoining restaurant.

'Who took my place?' she asked curiously, as she started on the warm goat's cheese salad she'd chosen to begin.

'Head office sent down a temporary replacement while I look round for a successor of your calibre,' said James, and changed the subject, asking if she'd seen the play currently running at the repertory theatre.

'No,' she confessed. 'My feet hurt so much I tend to loll about with a book or watch television in the evenings.'

James laid down his fork, and looked at her in the direct, searching way she knew so well. 'No trips to London?'

'None.' She returned the look steadily.

'Your relationship with Maynard is over?'

Eleri's eyes flashed. 'Very much so—though I

doubt one could describe what we had as a relationship, exactly. I met Toby through my friend, Vicky Mantle—the one who *still* works in Renshaw's. I go up to London for the weekend to stay with her fairly regularly, and she introduced me to Toby. He used to take me to the cinema, or clubbing now and again. But I always slept in Vicky's spare bed afterwards,' she added. And cursed herself silently for blurting out something so private.

James's eyes narrowed in surprise for a moment, but he introduced another subject deftly, and Eleri began to wonder when, if ever, he intended giving her the reason for their meeting. They were drinking coffee in a corner of one of the quieter bars after dinner, when he turned towards her on the padded bench seat and smiled wryly.

'You've been very patient, Eleri.'

'I have,' she agreed.

James nodded. 'All right. I won't beat about the bush. Head office has sent me a temporary assistant. Mrs Willis is a terrifying lady, about to retire, who is doing this as a great favour and never lets me forget the fact.'

'Oh?' Eleri eyed James warily. 'Have you done any interviews yet?'

He shook his head. 'No.'

Eleri looked long and hard into the light eyes which returned her scrutiny steadily, giving no clue to the thought processes behind them.

'Why not?' she asked at last.

'Because I'm determined to persuade you to come back to Northwold,' he informed her.

'I can't do that,' she said quietly, and refilled their cups with a steady hand.

'You're not even surprised I asked.'

'What other reason would you have for asking me out to dinner?'

He frowned. 'The same reason any man asks you out, I imagine—for the pleasure of your company.'

Eleri's heart skipped a beat. 'But in our case it's rather different.'

'Not really. You were a large part of my life for over twelve months, Eleri, and I've missed you like hell. Not just because you're so good at your job, either. Until the advent of Mrs Willis, who never wears anything other than a navy blue twin set and matching shapeless skirt, I never appreciated your faultless taste in clothes.'

'Thank you,' she said, surprised to discover James had ever noticed her appearance. 'I certainly never wear navy blue.'

'I thought not.' James subjected her to a comprehensive scrutiny. 'Tonight you look positively dazzling—more exotic and Italian, I suppose, with your hair loose.'

Eleri looked at him in astonishment, her heart suddenly hammering. To cover her shock she laughed a little, and drank down her coffee. 'You're misled by my colouring. My looks come from my Welsh mother. My father's fair.'

'Northern Italian?'

She nodded. 'The Veneto.'

James folded his arms across his chest, his eyes intent on her face. 'Eleri, are you refusing to come back because you don't want to, or because your pride won't allow it?'

Unlike her heart, Eleri's memory was in perfect working order. Her eyes gleamed coldly. 'I left under a cloud, if you remember. How could you possibly expect me to come back in the circumstances?'

'No one knows about your connection with Maynard other than my brother-in-law and myself.' He looked away across the bar. 'Sam told me Maynard obtained the information from someone at Merlin Ales. You're completely exonerated.'

'I want to be trusted, not exonerated,' she retorted.

'I do trust you. I told you that the day you walked out on me.' James paused, smiling crookedly. 'I didn't tell anyone you'd resigned, except for Bruce Gordon. The rest of the staff think you're taking some leave because your family needed you for a while.'

'They need me full stop,' she said flatly. 'So even if I wanted to come back I can't.'

'Ah, but you'd like to,' he said swiftly.

'All right. I would,' she admitted. 'I enjoyed my job. But I care too much for my family to take off again and leave them in the lurch.' Nor did she intend running back to Northwold just because James Kincaid crooked his finger and whistled. Much as she wanted to. She stood up. 'If you'd ask the waiter for my coat and call me a taxi it's time I went home. Busy day tomorrow.'

James signalled to a waiter. 'I'll drive you.'

'There's no need to go so far out of your way.'

'I literally pass your door.'

'You've moved from Compton Priors?'

'Yes. I never meant the cottage to be more than a stop-gap while I looked for something permanent. It actually belongs to my parents, so from now on I'll just use it as a weekend retreat now and again. I moved into a flat in town last week.' He helped her into her heavy gold wool jacket. 'Let's dash; it's started to snow again.' They went outside into a white, whirling night, and James rushed her over to his Land Rover Discovery and tossed her up into it, flakes of snow frosting his hair when he ran round to get in beside her. 'Brrr!' he complained, shivering. 'Weather like this spurred me into finding a flat. This winter I've had a couple of dicey journeys out to the cottage.'

The snow was coming down so thick and fast by the time they arrived in the town, Eleri told James to drop her at the end of the cul-de-sac.

'The house is at the end, so don't try and drive down—it's difficult to turn round,' she instructed, and James killed the engine.

'I shan't give up, Eleri. When you change your mind you know where to contact me.' He turned in his seat to look at her.

Eleri kept her eyes on the seat belt she was unfastening. 'I doubt that I will. But thanks for the meal. I'm afraid it was rather a wasted evening for you.'

'How could any time spent with you be wasted, Eleri?'

'You're very kind,' she said politely. 'I'm only sorry I had to disappoint you.'

'So am I.' He got out of the car and went round to help her out, then took her by surprise by clasping both her hands in his. 'Goodnight—but definitely not goodbye.'

CHAPTER THREE

NEXT day, over lunch, Eleri's family were full of curiosity about her evening—her mother, particularly, inquisitive about James Kincaid's motive for asking her out.

'If it was any other man, *cariad*, the reason would be obvious, but in the circumstances, you must admit it's a bit odd.'

'Perhaps he just fancies her,' said Nico, wolfing down large quantities of roast lamb. 'What's in this stuffing, Ma? It's different.'

'Laverbread, *cariad*,' said Catrin, and smiled at her mystified husband. 'Seaweed, of a sort, Mario. They've begun to get it in the market occasionally—sent up from Swansea.'

'Seaweed?' he said with professional interest. 'This is some Welsh recipe, no?'

'My mother used to do it this way,' she said, nodding. 'I'd forgotten about it until I read it in a magazine the other day. It's mixed with onion and breadcrumbs and a dash of orange juice. Do you like it?'

'It's magnificent!' said Mario with relish. 'We shall serve it in the restaurant.'

They were sitting round the oval table in the dining room for the midday meal always eaten together on

Sundays, at Catrin's insistence, since sometimes it was the only time in the week she could gather all her family together. Claudia and her husband Paul often came too, but today the weather was bad and the Contis were reduced to four, which centred squarely on Eleri's evening with James Kincaid.

'If you must know,' she said, resigned, 'Mr Kincaid took me out to dinner to try to persuade me to go back to my job at Northwold. It's my office skills he lusts after, not me.'

Her father gave her a startled, searching look. 'What did you say, *cara*?'

'I refused, of course.' She stood up to take their plates. 'I'll fetch the pudding.'

Her mother followed her out into the kitchen with the vegetable dishes. 'But you wanted to accept, love, didn't you?'

Eleri nodded. 'Yes. But don't worry. I wouldn't let you down like that. And it may be cutting my nose off to spite my face, but I've no intention of running back to Northwold at the drop of a hat. I do have my pride, Mother.'

'But you weren't really sacked.'

'No. But my integrity was questioned.' Eleri took a bowl of zabaglione from the fridge. 'Though I'm completely exonerated, James informed me.'

'James? On first-name terms now, then?'

'His idea, not mine.' Eleri smiled cajolingly at her mother. 'Shall I take the apple tart in, too? Zabaglione won't be enough for Nico.'

Later that night, Eleri was glad when the wedding supper had been served and she could escape from the restaurant to enjoy some time to herself at home. Sometimes she longed to join Vicky in London as her friend wanted. Until James Kincaid's arrival she'd tended to look on the Northwold post as a stepping-stone to some future high-powered job in the capital. But James's advent had put her ambitions on a back-burner, and now she was farther from realising them than ever before, involved in the family business after all, and likely to remain so for the foreseeable future.

The following week, to Eleri's intense irritation, she found herself looking up in anticipation every time a tall, dark man came into the coffee-shop. How could it be James during the week? she asked herself scornfully. Or any time at all. He'd done his persuading. He wouldn't ask again now she'd turned him down. She'd been foolish to accept his invitation to dinner. Her efforts at getting over him had been going rather well up to that point. Now, damn the man, she was back to square one.

One of the other duties Eleri had volunteered for, once she was working in the business, was to deliver meals ordered by customers wanting a full-scale dinner in the comfort of their own home. At first her father had demurred, saying it was better left with Luigi, the waiter who normally drove the small van and even served the meal if required. Luigi, however, had broken his ankle on an icy pavement during the unusually bitter cold spell, and Eleri was given reluctant permission to take over for him as a temporary measure.

'Anything to relieve the monotony, isn't it?' her mother had said, helping her load the van the first time. 'I thought you'd be glad to stay in on an evening after being on your feet all day.'

'It makes a change,' said Eleri cheerfully. 'Do they want me to serve this?'

'Certainly not,' said Catrin firmly. 'I don't mind you delivering a meal, but I'm not having my daughter stay to serve it.'

'I serve people all day in the coffee-shop,' Eleri pointed out.

'That's different,' said her mother, firmly illogical.

Eleri enjoyed taking over the delivery service. The meals were expensive, but none of the clients had complained to date, since the food was perfectly prepared and arrived ready to serve, other than for a little reheating of certain dishes.

A dinner for two had been ordered that night for an address in Chester Gardens.

'It is a very simple meal, *cara*,' said her father. 'But it is best you take the ingredients for the *insalata caprese* and make it up for the customer after you arrive. The main course is just pasta with meat sauce, so put it in a low oven while you make the salad, then come home. *Deo volente*, Luigi will be able to drive again soon.'

'But I like doing it, Pa,' she protested.

'I know.' He patted her cheek, then kissed it. 'Because you are bored, no?'

She grinned at him, put the containers in the car and slid behind the wheel, not troubling to contradict what was, her father knew well, the simple truth. She *was* bored. It was time she begged a Saturday off to spend a weekend with Vicky.

To Eleri's relief the address was a ground-floor apartment in one of the austerely beautiful Regency houses in Chester Gardens. Where a lift was involved the delivery was more complicated. She rang the bell, and after a short wait the panelled door swung open to reveal a tall, all too familiar figure.

James Kincaid stood transfixed at the sight of her. *'Eleri?'*

'Who is it?' called a voice in the background.

'The dinner you ordered,' he called back, looking embarrassed as he took one of the insulated containers from Eleri. 'The kitchen's along here.' He hurried a shell-shocked Eleri along the hall and into a high-ceilinged room with a black and white tiled floor and state-of-the-art equipment. He shut the door behind them and thrust a hand through his hair, his discomfiture so obvious Eleri forgot her own in her amusement.

'I apologise for this,' he said gruffly. 'Believe me. I had no idea.'

'Neither did I. Look, could I put the oven on for the main course, please?' she said, deliberately businesslike. 'Or you can put it in the microwave. I'm afraid I have to assemble the first course, but it won't take long. It's only a salad.'

'Please don't bother—I'm sure we can manage,' he said curtly. He went over to a large convector oven and switched it on. 'I'd better use this, I suppose. What temperature do I need?'

'Medium. But don't leave the dish in too long. Could I have a big round serving plate, please?'

James hunted in a cupboard and gave her a plate, then watched uneasily while Eleri sliced beef tomatoes and rounds of buffalo mozzarella cheese with the knife she'd brought with her. She arranged them in concentric circles on the plate, drizzled virgin olive oil over them, tore up a handful of fresh basil leaves and sprinkled them over the finished dish.

'There,' she said, smiling brightly. '*Insalata caprese.* Would you put it in the fridge, please? I'll leave you to slice the *focaccia* when you're ready to eat.' She unwrapped a flat loaf coated with onions and rosemary, then put the dish of pasta in the oven.

'Eleri—' began James.

'Please,' she said swiftly, 'just let me get away as quickly as possible.' She bit her lip, her face suddenly hot. 'Though I'm afraid you have to pay me first.'

James fished his wallet out from a back pocket and handed over the not inconsiderable sum required for his evening meal. Eleri took the money and gave him change, all in a silence so tangible it fairly simmered in the air.

'Normally one of our staff does this,' she said, not

looking at him. 'He's broken his ankle, so I'm filling in. If you order anything in future it's customary to give Luigi a tip.'

'For pity's sake, Eleri, I thought you'd black my eye if I offered *you* a tip!' He smiled ironically. 'It seems a totally inadequate and irrelevant thing to say, but thank you.'

'My pleasure,' fibbed Eleri dryly. 'Nice kitchen,' she added, then stiffened as the door opened and in came a tall, slender blonde in a dress Eleri had coveted in a glossy magazine.

'Dinner? How splendid. Wasn't I clever, James, to think of getting it sent in?' She smiled radiantly at Eleri and spoke loudly and very distinctly. 'Thank you so much. Do you speak English?'

Eleri was suddenly possessed by a demon. 'A leetle, *signorina*,' she said, avoiding James's stare. 'I 'ave prepare the *insalata*, and the pasta ees hotting in the oven.'

'Perfect. Have you paid her, James?'

'Yes,' he said, fixing Eleri with a cold, glittering stare. 'But I forgot to give her a tip.' He held out a five-pound note. 'Please accept this for your trouble, Signorina Conti.'

Serves me right, she thought, looking at it for a moment. She took it and smiled up at him with deliberate coquetry, then turned away with a swish of her hips. 'Mille *grazie*, Signor Kincaid. So kind.'

He ushered her out of the kitchen swiftly, closing the door behind him before almost propelling her along the hall. 'What the blazes got into you?' he growled.

'Sorry!' she whispered penitently. 'My schoolgirl sense of humour.' And one look at Camilla Tennent had rendered her mad with jealousy, but she wasn't telling him that. She slipped outside quickly as he opened the door, then gave him a mischievous smile over her shoulder. 'Enjoy your meal.'

It came as no surprise to Eleri to see a familiar figure enter the coffee-shop next morning. James took his place at table ten in the corner by the far window, but Eleri went on with her telephone conversation to the ice-cream supplier, making sure that James had already been served with coffee by the time she put the receiver down.

'The gentleman would like a word with you when you're free,' Luisa informed her, smiling all over her face. 'Why not take your break now? We can cope.'

Eleri poured herself a coffee and took it over to James's table, seating herself as he half rose. 'Are you acquiring a taste for our coffee?' she enquired.

'It's very good,' he agreed, 'but not the reason for my visit.'

'No. I didn't think it was.' Eleri smiled at him ruefully. 'Look, I'm sorry for last night. It was a stupid thing to do.'

'Actually it was very funny.' He smiled crookedly. 'I suppose it was a gut reaction to Camilla in her "speaking to foreigners" mode.'

'Partly.' She made a face. 'A bit embarrassing all round.'

'I came to explain that it wasn't my idea. Though to be fair I wouldn't have expected you to deliver the meal in person even if I'd known which restaurant Camilla chose.'

'My father only let me fill in for Luigi because I get a bit—' She stopped, biting her lip.

'Bored?' he prompted.

'Well, yes,' she admitted reluctantly.

'Good,' he said, surprising her. 'There's a simple solution. Come back to work at Northwold, Eleri. No—' He held up a hand. 'Hear me out. I know you turned me down flat last time, but was that because you really don't *want* to come back, or out of reluctance to make things difficult for your family?' His eyes held hers. 'Or was your pride hurt too badly to even think of coming back to Northwold?'

'Two out of three,' she said lightly, casting an eye round the rapidly filling coffee-shop. 'Look, I have to go.'

'Will you promise to think it over?'

Eleri stood up, and James followed suit. 'There's not much point.'

'Let me take you out to lunch tomorrow—' he began, but she shook her head.

'Sunday lunch is a sacred ritual in our household, I'm afraid. Besides,' she added, 'it won't make any difference. Goodbye.' Eleri gave him a friendly, impersonal smile and returned to her post, immersed in filling buns with ham and salad before James had even left the coffee-shop.

The rest of the day was difficult. Even though she was run off her feet, Eleri found it desperately hard to concentrate due to a burning desire to do as James asked and return to work at Northwold. But at the same time a cool, calculating voice in her brain wondered why he was so insistent on having her back. She had no illusions about being indispensable. There had to be dozens of other women, equally competent, only too eager to fill her shoes.

At last she bade Gianni and Luisa goodnight, and went through her nightly ritual of checking that all was ready for the next day, which this time, she thought with a sigh of thankfulness, wasn't until Monday morning, which was usually fairly quiet. She locked the front door, and was just about to look in on the restaurant when the phone rang in the nook behind the cash register.

'May I speak to Miss Conti?' said a familiar male voice.

'Speaking.'

'James here, Eleri. I'm having a few Northwold people round for an impromptu drinks party tomorrow night—Bruce and his wife, and a few of the others. No one had the chance to bid you a proper goodbye, so I thought it would be an excellent idea if you joined us for an hour or so.'

Eleri opened her mouth to say no, then paused. If she went to a drinks party designed as a sort of farewell to her, James would be forced to accept that she meant what she said about not going back to Northwold. It was too unsettling for words to hear him repeat the request she would never be able to accept—at least not until Nico was old enough to take over. And by that time James Kincaid would probably be chairman of the entire company, married to Camilla, and would have forgotten all about her.

'Are you still there, Eleri?'

'Is the party in your flat?'

'Yes. You know the address. Will you come?'

The prospect of Camilla Tennent as gracious hostess held little appeal, but on the other hand there was nothing to do tomorrow night other than watch television or read a book, or, if completely desperate, lend a hand in the trattoria to pass the time.

'Yes,' she said with sudden decision. 'Why not? I'll enjoy meeting the others again.'

'About seven, then? I'll look forward to it,' he said quickly.

'So will I.' Eleri put down the phone and leaned against the counter, staring across the darkened coffee-shop to the floodlit church across the cobbled square. She had kept quiet about her visit to Chester Gardens the night before, fairly sure her mother would have gone off like a rocket to hear she'd served dinner to James Kincaid. But her parents would look on a farewell party as a very nice touch, a fitting way to round off their clever daughter's time at Northwold. It would also reassure them that she meant what she said about staying to run the coffee-shop.

CHAPTER FOUR

ELERI parked her car in Chester Gardens at fifteen minutes past seven the following evening, frowning as she got out. James's Discovery was parked in the drive alongside the building, but there were no other cars around. Surely she wasn't the first to arrive? She drew the collar of her coat closer against the cold and rang the bell. She waited, then rang the bell again, seized with sudden doubt. Could she have mistaken the date? She was on the point of leaving when the door opened and she stared in horror at the sight of James in a dressing gown, red-eyed and shivering, his face deathly pale.

'Eleri?' he croaked, astonished. 'Didn't you get my message?'

'James! You look terrible.' She eyed him in consternation. 'What's this about a message?'

He beckoned her in, closing the door behind her. 'I woke up with a temperature this morning, so I rang round to cancel. I've got flu or something.'

There's nothing quite so embarrassing, thought Eleri, as arriving dressed to kill for a cancelled party. 'Get back to bed,' she said decisively. 'I'm sorry about this. When you rang me who took the message?'

'Someone young and male.'

'Nico—I'll kill him!' Eleri looked at James searchingly. 'Have you taken anything?'

He shook his head, swaying on his feet. 'Couldn't find anything to take.'

Eleri sighed. 'James, where's your bedroom?'

'Downstairs,' he said, shivering convulsively. 'And I'd better get back there. Sorry about this, Eleri.'

She hesitated for a moment, then seized his arm. 'Come on, I think I'd better see you safely back to bed.'

To her surprise, James made only a token protest as she accompanied him down the stairs. Eleri's concern deepened as the feverish heat from his body penetrated right through the heavy wool of her coat. He waved a hand towards a door which opened into a large, lamplit room, and she steered James towards a vast, velvet armchair and pushed him down into it, then turned her attention to the tangled chaos of the bed.

'Where do you keep your bedlinen?' she asked, and he stared at her uncomprehendingly. 'James,' she said patiently, 'your bed's like a rats' nest. So tell me where you keep your sheets, then have a hot shower while I change your bed. You'll feel better afterwards.'

'I can't possibly let you do this!' he protested hoarsely.

'No "letting" about it,' she said inexorably. 'Come on—don't argue.'

His eyes lit with a fleeting gleam of amusement. 'Shrew!' He broke off to cough, waving an arm towards the door. 'Airing cupboard—hall,' he wheezed.

Eleri stood over him while he dragged himself out of the chair and made his way unsteadily towards a door in the corner of the room. Outside in the small passageway, after opening a couple of wrong doors, she found an airing cupboard with neatly stacked Egyptian cotton sheets, spare blankets and, best of all, a quilt.

This wasn't how she'd anticipated spending the evening, she thought wryly as she stripped James's bed. She remade it with crisp, fresh sheets, added an extra blanket and the quilt, plumped up the newly covered pillows, then gathered up the discarded linen and took it out into the hall to dispose of later. When she went back into James's room he was leaning in his bathroom doorway, shivering.

'I'm cold. I think I'd better wear pyjamas,' he croaked through chattering teeth.

'Where are they?'

'In the chest. Third or fourth drawer down. Haven't seen them for a while.' He tried to smile, and Eleri wondered if she ought to call a doctor. She found the pyjamas, handed them to him, then told him to get himself to bed while she made him a hot drink.

'Have you had anything to eat today?' she asked, and he shook his head.

'Not hungry.'

Eleri went upstairs to the kitchen to find that James,

unlike Toby, was obviously in the habit of catering for himself. He had plentiful supplies of basic necessities in the refrigerator, and a large pottery bowl on the kitchen table was piled high with fruit, including, she saw with satisfaction, some limes and lemons—ready, presumably, for the drinks at the cancelled party. When a brief search through well-stocked cupboards yielded up a can of beef consommé, Eleri decanted it into a large china beaker and put it in James's microwave. While it was heating she went along the hall to a sitting room where, as she'd anticipated, she found a table with a tray of decanters and bottles. Eleri took a swift, covetous look at deep, comfortable chairs and heavy, striped linen curtains, sighing as she eyed a vivid seascape over the fireplace. Yet another flat she'd give her eye-teeth for.

Back in the kitchen, she made a pot of tea, toasted a slice of wholemeal bread and buttered it sparsely, doctored the soup with a generous helping of sherry, found a large bottle of mineral water and put everything on a tray to take down to James.

He was propped up in bed, pale, hollow-eyed, and obviously feeling wretched. 'Eleri,' he rasped in consternation, as she set the tray down on a table beside him, 'You shouldn't have done all this. A damn nuisance you never got my message.'

'Perhaps it's just as well. At least it means I've been able to sort you out a bit.' She thrust extra pillows behind him. 'There, sit up a little and drink this soup. The fever's depressing your appetite, but you need liquid. Try to eat some toast, though. And could I have your front door key, please? I need to pop out to get some medication for you.'

He eyed her blankly. 'Medication?' He breathed in sharply, then began to cough, and Eleri dived to relieve him of the tray until the spasm was over.

'I'd better leave this on the table. I don't know where you keep your napkins, so I just brought you some kitchen paper. And don't forget to drink your tea.'

'Lord, you're bossy,' he wheezed.

'Efficient, not bossy! Shan't be long.'

'Keys on the dressing table,' he said, and drank some of the soup, then smiled. 'This is good.'

'Drink all of it,' she ordered. 'I'll be about fifteen minutes.'

James looked at her as though he were seeing her for the first time. 'Great dress, Eleri.'

'A bit inappropriate in the circumstances,' she said dryly.

Eleri drove back home, relieved to find it still deserted, then collected whatever she could find by way of flu remedies. Armed with painkillers and decongestant capsules, she collected a large box of tissues from her bedroom, then drove back to Chester Gardens, smiling to herself as she unlocked James's door. Camilla Tennent would probably be mad as fire if she knew someone else was ministering to him. Not that Eleri could picture the decorative Camilla changing sheets and knocking up nourishing snacks.

When Eleri hurried down into James's room, to her deep dismay he sat bolt upright, staring at her with glassy, uncomprehending eyes.

'What the hell are you doing here?' he demanded, his voice so hoarse it was almost unrecognisable.

Eleri marched purposefully to the bed. 'Sorry to leave you alone. I just went home for some pills.'

'Eleri? Is Bruce there? Call a meeting of the block managers—' He broke off, coughing.

She put a hand on his forehead and bit her lip. He was burning up. She stacked the pillows tidily and urged him back down against them, then pulled up the covers. 'I'm just going upstairs to get you a cold drink.' She touched his hand, wincing at the heat of it. 'Try to lie still.'

Eleri went from the room swiftly and raced upstairs to the telephone in the hall. She rang the emergency number of the family doctor and told the answering service that Mr James Kincaid of Flat One, 3 Chester Gardens, needed medical attention. She described his symptoms, stressed the delirium, and put the phone down.

When she got back James was shivering, with red patches of colour along his cheekbones, but this time, to her relief, he looked at her with recognition.

'I've called a doctor,' she said militantly. 'And no protests, please.'

'I wouldn't dare,' he croaked, and swallowed with difficulty. 'I'm very thirsty.'

'Right. Have some mineral water. I'll make you a

fruit drink later on.' She filled a glass and handed it to him. 'James, is there someone I could ring to come and look after you?'

James drained the glass, then subsided, shaking his head. 'Absolutely not. I've got a cold and a bit of a cough, that's all—nothing to make a fuss about. In any case, my parents live in France and my sister's got three children under ten.'

Eleri bit her lip, frowning. 'I could ring Miss Tennent, perhaps.'

'Camilla?' He laughed, but it quickly changed to a bout of coughing. 'Mention flu and she'd run a mile.'

'Who, then? You really shouldn't be alone in the state you're in,' said Eleri, worried.

'I'll be fine,' he assured her.

Unconvinced, Eleri took the used sheets upstairs and put them in the washing machine she found in the small room leading off the kitchen. Afterwards she squeezed lemons and limes to make a drink to leave for James overnight. When she took it down to him he was dozing, his breathing so stertorous her concern deepened. She drew a chair up to the bed and sat down, more and more convinced she should stay the night to look after him.

Eleri was very glad to let the doctor in soon afterwards. He was young, wearily cheerful, and reassuring. 'You've got a dose of good old-fashioned influenza, Mr Kincaid, plus a respiratory infection, which is rocketing your temperature,' he announced after a very thorough examination of the invalid. 'But normally you're obviously very fit, so you'll soon throw it off. I'll give your wife a prescription for some antibiotics for the chest infection.' He smiled at Eleri, told her which pharmacy stayed open late on Sundays, congratulated her on her common sense in providing painkillers and fruit drinks, and emphasised the importance of taking the antibiotics at regular intervals, including through the night for the preliminary doses. Eleri saw him out, then went back downstairs.

'So much for your bit of a cold!' she said grimly to James. 'Be good for a few minutes, please. I'm just going down to the town to get your prescription.'

'You shouldn't be wearing yourself out with all this,' he said bitterly.

'Nonsense. It's a good thing I'm here.'

'From my point of view it's wonderful—madam wife!'

Eleri smiled. 'Now try to sleep. I'll be back as soon as I can.'

She drove down to the chemist for the medication, and arrived back to find James on his way back to bed from the bathroom. She straightened the sheets quickly, plumped up the pillows and pulled the covers over James when he stretched out thankfully.

'I had to get out,' he said with mock contrition. 'Some things you can't do for me.'

'True.' Unembarrassed, she handed him the first dose of pills and a glass of water. 'But this I can. Swallow the pills and every drop of this water to safeguard your kidneys.'

James eyed her balefully over the rim of the glass. 'A beautiful woman in my bedroom and she discusses my kidneys! I must be losing my touch.'

Eleri grinned, and looked at her watch.

'Are you going?' he said in alarm.

She shook her head. 'I was just checking the time. It's nine-fifteen.'

'Is that all? It feels like midnight.'

'Your next dose is due at one-fifteen.' She came to a decision. 'James, could I use your phone?'

'You can do anything you want,' he said hoarsely, his bloodshot eyes gleaming suddenly. 'I was mad to let you go.'

'You're rambling again,' she said prosaically. 'I'll be back in a minute.'

Eleri ran upstairs and rang home. 'Nico? Is Ma home?'

'No, not yet.'

'Right. Now listen carefully. Give her a message— and don't forget it like the one you forgot to give me today, you monster.'

He said something Catrin would have boxed his ears for. '*Sorry*, El. Mr Kincaid rang the house this morning, only I was on my way out and I forgot—' He groaned. 'Are you *very* mad at me?'

'Do I ever stay mad at you? I could have strangled you earlier on, though. Take this number down, and ask Ma to ring me as soon as she can. It's very important, love.'

He promised faithfully to tell his mother the moment she came through the door. 'Would you rather I asked her on her own, El?'

Eleri chuckled. 'It might be a good idea at that.'

'Not in any bother, are you?' he demanded. 'Just say the word.'

'No, no. Nothing wrong—I'm fine,' she assured him, touched. 'Just tell Ma to ring.'

When she got back to him James frowned at her in disapproval. 'You should be going home,' he said hoarsely.

'It's early yet.' She smiled. 'Though I *am* rather hungry. If you don't mind I'll just pop upstairs and make myself a sandwich.'

'Hell, yes,' he said in remorse. 'I should have thought—'

'You're not well enough to think,' she said cheerfully. 'How do you feel?'

His mouth twisted. 'Manly pride prompts me to say I'm fine. But to be honest, Eleri, I feel grim.'

Not that he needed to tell her. His deep-set eyes were over-bright, and his skin still burned to the touch when she laid her hand on his forehead.

'Once the medication gets to work you should begin to feel better,' she said soothingly. 'Have a rest now. I'll be back down once I've eaten something. And don't try to answer your phone when it rings; I'm waiting for a phone-call from my mother.'

Eleri had eaten a cheese sandwich and was making herself a cup of coffee when her mother finally rang.

'Eleri? Is that you?'

'Yes.'

'What number is this? Where are you? Nico says the party you were going to was cancelled—'

'It was. James Kincaid's gone down with a bad dose of flu. I'm at his flat.' Eleri explained the situation swiftly and succinctly, including the lack of immediate relations to help. 'I don't know what to do, Mamma. James is really quite ill—even delirious at times. Someone should be on hand to give him his medication through the night.'

'There's no one else at all?' demanded her mother. 'No girlfriend, even?'

'Oh, yes. But in London, not here—and not too keen where germs are involved, I gather.'

'And you're on hand.' Catrin sighed. 'All this means you feel obliged to stay with him, I suppose.'

'I do, really, Ma. He's got a raging temperature.'

There was silence on the line for a moment. 'Eleri, I know you won't rest if you leave the poor man alone in that state. And it was very sweet of you to consult with me first. You don't need permission at your age. I'll send Nico over with your things. He can stay the night with you.'

'*What?*'

'Calm down. I know you don't need a chaperon, girl. But if Mr Kincaid gets delirious again you might be glad of a man to help you.' There was a pause. 'Humour me. Nico can sleep on a sofa, and get off to school straight from there in the morning.'

Eleri knew her mother was talking sense. 'Oh, all

right. But for pity's sake feed Nico first, please,' she implored.

'Of course I will. And I'll take over at the coffee-shop for you tomorrow too,' added her mother. 'You'll be too tired.'

'I hadn't even thought that far! Bless you,' said Eleri fervently. 'This all came as a surprise. If Nico had given me the message I'd never have known James was ill.'

'Is he very bad, *cariad*?'

'It's a nasty dose of flu—with a bad chest, aches and pains, the lot. He looks ghastly, but normally he's pretty fit. Once the antibiotics start to work he'll improve fast enough.'

'In which case get back to your own bed tomorrow and rest. You probably won't sleep much tonight.'

'Thanks again, Mamma. You're an angel.'

James woke some time later, to find Eleri curled up in his huge crimson velvet armchair reading, the light from the lamp falling on her face.

'Study in velvet—by Raphael, possibly.' He smiled at her startled look. 'I thought you'd be gone by now. What time is it?'

'Half ten.' She braced herself. 'James, I'm going to stay here tonight, to make sure you take your pills.'

He looked stunned. 'But I can't let you do that—'

'Don't worry. Your reputation's safe. I hope you don't object, but Nico's coming round to spend the night in your spare bed.'

James grinned. 'In case I get out of hand? At the

moment I'm no danger to your virtue, Eleri—much as I'd like to be,' he added, starting to cough. 'And of course I don't object.'

'You were delirious earlier on,' she said matter-of-factly. 'If you start ranting again I might need help.'

'I would never hurt you!' he panted, shocked.

'I know. But you're bigger than me. If you need helping back to bed I might be glad of Nico's muscles.' Eleri looked up at the sound of a bell. 'That must be him now.'

She went upstairs and let Nico in, telling him to stow his bicycle in the hallway, preferably without marking the wall.

He looked round with a whistle of appreciation. 'Not bad!' His eyes narrowed. 'Are you all right, El? You look done in.'

'The bedrooms are downstairs; I've been running up and down quite a bit. Sorry about all this, love.'

'I don't mind defending your honour!' he assured her, grinning.

Eleri shook her head, laughing. 'Are those Ma's instructions?'

'No, Pop's. Not in so many words, but I got the drift.' His eyes gleamed wickedly. 'If you don't want your honour defended I'll keep out of the way.'

'The question doesn't arise. But if I do I can cope very well without help!' she said tartly, and relieved him of a large overnight bag. 'I hope Ma put something practical in here. For a ministering angel I'm a tad overdressed.'

'She put a lot of stuff in, including my blazer.' Nico sprang to attention and saluted. 'I must hang it up immediately, be helpful, and no staying up all night watching television, mind,' he chanted, with a wickedly accurate Welsh lilt.

Eleri giggled and took out the neatly folded blazer to find toilet things, underwear, jeans, a white shirt, her yellow sweater, some thick tights and a pair of flat black loafers—and at the bottom of the bag a biscuit tin full of Catrin's famous Welshcakes. She beckoned to Nico. 'I'll show you where to sleep. Hang up your blazer in the spare room, then you'd better meet James. If I do need help with him at any point he might as well get to know your face first.'

James looked up with interest when Eleri ushered the tall, good-looking youngster into the room.

'James, this is Nico,' she announced with a hint of pride.

'The chaperon, I assume,' said James, with a hoarse chuckle.

Nico grinned. 'Eleri's minder.'

'Totally unnecessary,' she said tartly. 'My mother thought I might need help if you—er—'

'Got familiar with my nurse,' said James blandly, and Nico chortled.

'If your temperature rises and you get delirious again,' contradicted Eleri crossly, and waved a hand at Nico. 'Off you go, love, or you might catch James's bug.'

'Right. Goodnight, Mr Kincaid.'

'James, please.'

Nico put up a thumb in smiling acknowledgement and went bounding upstairs to watch James's television.

Eleri sat down in the chair near the bed. 'How are you feeling, James?'

'Every bone aches, my head's on fire and it hurts to breathe,' he said bitterly. '*And* I feel guilty as hell.'

'Why?'

'Because you, not your impressive kid brother, will inevitably catch whatever it is I've got!' He glared at her, coughing, and Eleri got up to fill a glass with fruit juice.

'Too late to worry about that now. Would you prefer a hot drink?' she asked when the paroxysm subsided.

James drank thirstily, then put the glass down. 'I'd *prefer* you to go home and leave me to it,' he croaked irascibly. 'I'm perfectly capable of swallowing a couple of pills now and then.'

'Right,' she said promptly. 'Where's your alarm clock?'

He eyed her suspiciously. 'Alarm clock?'

She nodded. 'So I can set it for one-fifteen. But when you take the pills you must remember to reset the clock for five-fifteen, and then again for nine-fifteen, and so on. And if you perspire and drench your sheets again, please change them at once. I'll leave fresh bedlinen on the armchair when I go—'

'OK—you've made your point.' He slumped

against the pillows, defeated. 'But I'm worried about you.'

'I'm never ill,' she assured him.

'Neither am I, normally. But this bug's been rampaging through Northwold—Bruce was off for a week with it.' His heavy eyes met hers. 'Though I didn't miss him nearly as much as I miss you, Eleri.'

Her velvet-covered heart gave a thump. 'I've missed my job too,' she said coolly. 'And now I'm going to change this dress for something more practical and blow the whistle on Nico. He's got school in the morning.'

James smiled. 'He's quite a lad—must be a serious danger to the local maidens.'

'For the moment, surprisingly, he's more interested in football.' Eleri smiled ruefully. 'He's also a walking appetite, so I'm sure you won't mind if I make him a sandwich. What can I get for you at the same time?'

James coughed dryly. 'I'm not hungry. But I'm tired of my own company. If you feel the damage from infection is done by now, would you make a pot of tea and share it with me down here?'

'Of course.'

'Eleri,' he said, as she got up to go, 'I laid in quite a stock of non-alcoholic stuff for my little soiree, plus nuts and potato chips and so on. Tell Nico to help himself.'

'He'll be your friend for life!'

CHAPTER FIVE

ELERI changed her clothes in the spare bedroom, then ran Nico to earth in front of a television in what was obviously James's study. An open, bulging briefcase lay on a swivel chair behind a large desk littered with paperwork, and a side table held a computer, printer, and the inevitable fax machine.

'Neat room, this,' said Nico. 'How's the invalid?'

'Fretting in case I catch his flu. I'm going to make tea,' she added. 'James said to help yourself to drinks.'

Nico shot up to follow her to the kitchen, and returned to his film armed with a can of diet cola and a vast bag of potato chips.

Eleri made a pot of tea, put white silver-rimmed mugs on a tray, added a plate of her mother's Welshcakes, and went downstairs to James, who raised an eyebrow at her change of clothes.

'I've never seen you in jeans. You look cute.'

'Cute!' She pulled a face and sat down to pour tea. 'My mother sent some Welshcakes over. Would you like one?'

James eyed the plate she was offering, but with reluctance shook his head. 'Eleri, I don't think I do. Don't tell your mother,' he added hoarsely.

'Don't worry, I won't. But drink your tea,' she said sternly. 'You really must keep up your fluid intake.'

'Yes, Nurse,' he said meekly. 'What's Nico doing?'

'Stretched out on a sofa in your study with a fix of junk food, eyes glued to a Western.' She eyed him curiously. 'Why all the diet cola, by the way?'

'Camilla's tipple.'

Eleri turned her attention to the books on the bedside table. 'Have you read all these?'

'No. I had a go earlier with the thriller, but my eyes are full of sand. They can't cope.'

'I could read to you,' she offered.

James looked at her in surprise. 'Would you really do that?'

'Yes, if you'd like me to.'

'Does this mean you're going to stay in here all night with me?'

'I won't if you'd rather I didn't,' she said quickly.

'Eleri, of course I'd like you to stay. But it's too much to ask!'

'It's just for tonight.' She looked him in the eye. 'To be honest, you look rough, James. Besides, thanks to my mother, Nico will be in the spare bed. I need to dose you at one, then afterwards I'll curl up in this glorious chair for the night. I'll be fine.'

He settled himself lower in the bed, wincing as he stretched his aching limbs. 'I know I should argue, Eleri, but I don't feel up to it at the moment.'

'One always feels worse at night,' she assured him,

and picked up the book. 'I'll start from the beginning.'

The young Eleri had gained practice in the art of reading aloud when Nico was small. Her low-pitched voice was very expressive, and the thriller she chose gripped from the first page, making it easy for her to read with animation. James lay motionless, watching her as he listened. Her hair, as usual, had two thick front strands thrust behind her ears, and shone like ebony in the muted light which lent a tinge of colour to her absorbed face.

Eleri knew James was watching her, but after the first page or two forgot about the unwavering grey eyes as she concentrated on the convolutions of the plot. At one stage Nico put his head round the door and waved a silent goodnight. James raised a hand in return, and Eleri smiled affectionately as she went on with her reading. Out of the corner of her eye she could see James's long body outlined beneath the bedclothes, and at first he shifted restlessly from time to time, unable to control the occasional cough. But after a while he grew quieter, and by midnight he was asleep. Eleri put the book down and curled up in the chair, yawning. She checked that the alarm on her watch was set for James's next dose of medication and closed her eyes in an effort to get some sleep herself.

She woke with a start, feeling cramped and stiff, and very cold, despite the warmth of the room. She got up to look at James, who was lying on his back,

breathing heavily, his face flushed. He moved restlessly and flung out an arm, muttering incoherently.
A look at her watch confirmed that it was almost time
for his pills. Eleri touched his hot, dry hand gently.

'James,' she whispered. 'Time to wake up.'

His eyelids flew open and he stared blankly into her face, then heaved himself up. 'Who—?
What—?'

'It's only me, James,' she said briskly, secretly dis-
mayed by his blank, staring eyes. 'It's time to take
your medicine.'

'Bathroom,' he muttered, and staggered from the
bed to weave his way across the room, banging the
bathroom door behind him.

Nico came racing in, wearing a black and white
Juventus football shirt and brief boxer shorts. 'Eleri,
is he all right?'

'I don't know,' she said tightly. 'Pity I had to wake
him, but it's time for his antibiotics. See if he's all
right, love.'

Nico crossed the room to knock on the door. 'Mr
Kincaid—James. Are you OK?' He threw an uncer-
tain look at Eleri. 'Shall I barge in?'

'Yes, please.'

Nico opened the door and let out such a howl of
dismay Eleri pushed him aside to find James semi-
conscious on the floor.

'James,' she rapped out. 'Wake up.'

His eyes opened, looking up in bewilderment at the
two anxious faces bent over him. 'What happened?'

'You keeled over,' said Eleri. 'Nico, you take one arm, I'll take the other.' With difficulty, since James's legs seemed unwilling to support him, they manoeuvred him to his feet and stood him upright, with an arm around each of their shoulders. 'Do you need to stay in the bathroom on your own for a moment?' panted Eleri. 'Or can we get you back to bed?'

James thought it over. 'Back to bed, please.'

Eleri was heartily glad of Nico's help as they got James to the armchair and sat him in it while she tidied the bed. They heaved James out of the chair again and got him back into the bed, both of them breathless by the time James was neatly tucked up against the pillows.

'Could you hang on here a minute, Nico, while I go upstairs for more mineral water?' asked Eleri.

'You stay. I'll get it,' he said, and sprinted from the room.

Eleri sat on the edge of the bed and took James's hand. 'How do you feel?'

'Not so hot,' he admitted. 'Sorry about all that. Damn good thing Nico was here. Great kid, isn't he?'

Eleri nodded, deeply worried by the febrile heat of the hand she was holding. Added to the glitter in the sunken grey eyes it told a very disquieting story. She looked up with a determined smile as Nico came back with a large bottle of mineral water and fresh glasses.

'I've put the kettle on, El. I thought you'd want tea.'

'Thanks, love. You're a star.'

James eyed the boy ruefully. 'Sorry about all this, friend. Don't hang about here, though.'

Nico grinned. 'I've already had flu, before Christmas. That's why Eleri's such an ace nurse. She practised on me.' He yawned suddenly. 'But I suppose I'd better get back to bed. Double maths first thing in the morning!' With a melodramatic shudder he went from the room.

'Right,' said Eleri briskly. 'Time for your pills.'

James swallowed them obediently, but baulked at the entire glass of water. 'I'll have to go to the bathroom again. And look what happened last time!'

'Never mind. All the water, please.'

He groaned, but obeyed her, gasping for air as he gave the glass back to her. 'Tyrant!'

'Just following doctor's orders,' she said, unmoved. 'Now try to sleep. I'm just going up to the kitchen to make myself some tea. Don't move. I won't be long.'

Eleri took advantage of the brief respite to visit the guest bathroom herself, where she brushed her teeth and washed her face in an effort to perk herself up. She made herself a mug of tea, peeped in the guest room to find Nico was already fast asleep again, then went back to James.

'Shall I read to you again?' she asked as she curled up in the armchair.

James shook his head. 'Talk to me for a while instead. You're cold,' he added accusingly as she shivered a little.

'The tea will warm me up.'

'Go and get some blankets,' ordered James, 'and have some of these pillows.'

Eleri got up. 'No need. I'll get some from the bed in the other room.'

Five minutes later Eleri was comfortably settled in the chair in a cocoon of blankets, a pillow from the guest room behind her head, suddenly struck by the improbability of the situation.

'Why the little smile?' enquired James. Eleri explained, and he chuckled. 'I never dreamed I'd be so lucky!' He sobered abruptly. 'But what about tomorrow? You'll be fit to drop after this.'

'My mother's filling in for me.'

James swore under his breath. 'She must be cursing me.'

'No. She quite understood that I couldn't abandon you on your bed of pain.'

'Did your father understand too?' he asked dryly.

Eleri grinned. 'I wouldn't take bets on *that*.'

'I don't blame him. If I had a daughter like you I doubt I'd be very happy with the situation either.'

'Nonsense,' said Eleri promptly. 'You're ill, and I just happened to be on hand. Anyone else would do the same.'

'I seriously doubt it,' he retorted. 'You're a one-off, Eleri Conti. Before I even arrived at the Gloucestershire brewery George Reeder told me I was lucky to get you. I hadn't been there a day before I knew exactly what he meant.'

'Which didn't keep you from suspecting me when

the takeover was leaked,' she retorted, unable to keep a biting note from her voice.

'I knew there had to be some logical explanation.' He smiled bitterly. 'I never had the least intention of firing you. Only a fool would have dispensed with services like yours, Eleri. You smoothed my path enormously during those first few weeks as MD.' His eyes locked with hers. 'I've been like a lost soul since you walked out on me.'

Although this was hard to imagine, his words were balm to Eleri's soul. 'It's nice to know I was missed.'

'Tell me the truth,' he demanded. 'If you could, would you like to come back to Northwold?'

'Oh, yes,' she said without hesitation.

'But you won't desert your family.'

'No, I won't. But that's not the only reason.' She looked James in the eye. 'Your suspicions hurt. Badly.'

He winced, his eyes glittering in his colourless face. 'And you can't forgive me?'

'Exactly.'

'Would it make any difference if I grovelled?'

Eleri shook her head, smiling reluctantly. 'No, it wouldn't. Nor can I picture you grovelling—any more than I can see you as a lost soul.' She gave a sudden, involuntary yawn.

'You must be exhausted,' said James grimly.

'No. Just tired. We're both tired,' said Eleri firmly. 'Do you need anything?'

'Nothing at all—other than an end to this blasted bug.'

'Which will come all the sooner if you rest.'

'Yes, Nurse,' he said meekly.

She chuckled. '*Very* good. You're learning. I'm going to turn out the light now.'

'Pity. I like looking at you.'

'Try to sleep, please.' Eleri switched off the lamp and settled deeper into her nest of blankets, wishing she could have kept the light on to read. Wakeful in the silent darkness, she recognised only too plainly what a rash undertaking this was. But no way could she have handed James over to some nursing service, as she should have done.

Her family obviously thought her mad to volunteer her own services to the man responsible for her resignation from her job. And she could see their point of view. But it had been worth it to learn how much he regretted his part in that, and wanted her back. But it would be worse than rash to return to work for a man she was still in love with. If she'd persuaded herself she no longer cared for him, her frantic anxiety about his illness had set her straight on that score. Very clearly. And even if he had genuinely missed her at Northwold, the fact remained that James Kincaid's private life belonged to Miss Camilla Tennent.

Eleri sat very still, alert to any noise from the bed. And for a long time James lay quiet, his breathing harsh but regular as he slept at last. But after a while he began to flail about in the bed, muttering, and she switched on the light to see blankets and quilt lying half off the bed.

She left her chair, and stealthily, trying not to wake him, pulled the sheet into place, and anchored the blanket and quilt more securely. The sheet was damp, and his forehead was beaded with perspiration. Eleri hung over him, desperately worried. He was obviously burning up again. Suddenly his eyes flew open and stared at her blankly for a second, then lit with sudden heat.

Without warning James pulled her down to him and held her in an iron-hard embrace, impeding her frantic opposition very effectively by rolling on top of her and smothering her protests with a hot, masterful mouth as he kissed her in a way which demonstrated only too plainly that kisses were only the preliminaries for what he had in mind.

Only he wasn't *in* his right mind, she reminded herself, struggling frantically. He was obviously delirious again. Which just wasn't fair. Her efforts failed ignominiously, because James seemed possessed with manic strength. His body kept hers captive by sheer superiority of size and weight, his mouth and tongue so wildly importunate that her traitorous body began to respond to him—all her secret fantasies about James realised, caution forgotten as he held her close. His mouth and hands ignited flames which raged out of control, his clever, relentless fingers hot on her skin as he wrought such turbulent magic she was helpless in the thrall of sensations which surpassed the most vivid of her fantasies. As she writhed, gasping, beneath him he made a smothered, relishing noise against her mouth. Then his shaking hands were fumbling at her belt and the spell was broken. Cold, prudent sanity came rushing back in force.

Mortified by her reckless, uninhibited surrender, Eleri forced herself to go limp for an instant, then gave a sudden, violent heave which precipitated her over the side of the bed into a sprawling heap on the floor. For a moment she stayed there, her body vibrating with her still clamouring senses, then she scrambled awkwardly to her feet to face James, who was kneeling on the bed, his appalled eyes wide with shock.

Eleri tugged down her sweater, thrust her tumbled hair out of her eyes and manhandled James back against the pillows.

'Eleri, I thought I was dreaming,' he said through chattering teeth. 'What can I say? I'm hellish sorry. Did I—hurt you?'

'No.' She let out a long, shaky breath. 'You didn't know me.'

James's eyes met hers. 'I really did think I was dreaming. But I knew it was you.'

Shaken and crimson-faced, Eleri took a look at her watch. A while to go yet before his next medication. 'If you can make it unaided to the bathroom,' she said unevenly, 'I'll change the bed. You've been perspiring pretty freely.'

'Sweating like a pig, you mean.'

'Try to stand up.'

James got to his feet with care, and professed himself able to manage unaided.

'Don't have a shower this time,' she ordered, and went to the chest for a fresh pair of pyjamas. 'Just rub yourself down with a bathtowel and put these on.'

He took them from her, eyeing her morosely, and headed for the bathroom. Eleri stripped the bed as quickly as she could manage with trembling hands, and remade it just in time for James to slide, shivering, between the covers.

'I wish my thermostat would start working properly,' he said irascibly. 'I'm either freezing or at boiling point. Is it time for more pills?'

'Not quite yet. Don't worry, I'll wake you,' she assured him.

'And if I go berserk again hit me over the head with a book,' he ordered as Eleri settled back into her nest of blankets. 'I'm hellish sorry I frightened you.'

'You didn't frighten me, exactly.' Which was true enough. It was her own behaviour which had scared her witless, not his. 'No harm done. Try to sleep.'

'What if I attack you again?'

'I'll be better prepared next time. But there won't be a next time. Would you like me to read to you again?'

James shook his head, eyeing her closely. 'You've got circles under your eyes.'

'So have you.' She smiled. 'Don't worry. I'm tired,

not ill. I'm as strong as a horse.' Which she devoutly hoped would be proved true, because it would be nothing short of a miracle if she escaped infection, one way and another.

'Talk to me,' he commanded, sliding lower in the bed. 'Tell me about yourself. Has it been hard, Eleri, to make such a change in your life?'

'Harder than I expected,' she admitted, glad of a less inflammatory topic of conversation. 'Don't misunderstand I love my family. But running the coffee-shop doesn't stretch me the way the Northwold job did.' She smiled ruefully. 'Nor can I get away so easily. These days I need a special dispensation to get to London for a weekend.'

He frowned. 'Life must be a touch on the quiet side for you.'

Eleri nodded. 'But I'll get used to it. At least my parents are happy. I used to talk about getting a job in London, which my typically Latin father found hard to take. He'd prefer me to copy my sister Claudia. She didn't leave home until she married.'

James smiled. 'Not your idea of a good move, I take it.'

'No.' She looked at her watch. 'Right. I think you can take your pills now.'

James groaned. 'Which means half a gallon of water again, I suppose?'

'Absolutely.' Eleri stood over him while he drank it down, then ordered him off to the bathroom again.

'Have you thought of joining the army?' he demanded bitterly as he slid out of bed. 'You'd make a great sergeant major.'

'Don't be ungrateful.' She held out a dressing gown. 'Here, put this on.'

He glared at her, but slid his arms into it and made for the bathroom—looking, she noted, brightening, a lot steadier than before. She tidied the bed quickly, turned back a corner of the sheet neatly, then wrapped herself in her blankets and curled up in the chair before James came back to get into bed.

'You didn't wait to tuck me up,' he said accusingly.

Eleri smiled sweetly. 'Since I'm neither your nanny nor an army sergeant I decided you could manage that by yourself. I think you're on the mend.'

'No, I'm not,' he said instantly. 'I need a lot more tender, loving care.'

'This is a one-off tonight, James. Tomorrow you can fend for yourself.' She laughed at his look of dismay. 'I've got a job to do.'

'I know,' he said morosely. 'And it isn't even with me at Northwold.'

'No,' she agreed, suddenly depressed. 'It isn't. Goodnight, James. Try to sleep.' And to call a halt to any more talking she switched off the light.

To Eleri's surprise she slept quite heavily, despite the confines of the chair, and woke with a start when her watch alarm went off at five-fifteen. All was quiet in the room as she got up stiffly to check on the invalid. James was sleeping very tidily, all the covers neatly drawn up to his chin. He looked pale and hollow-cheeked, the dark stubble along his jaw no help to his appearance, but despite the dark rings under his closed eyes he looked better. His lids shot up as she bent over him, his eyes lighting up at the sight of her.

'Hi,' he said hoarsely.

'Hi, yourself.' Eleri straightened, pushing her hair behind her ears. 'How do you feel?'

James thought for a moment. 'I'm not up to running a marathon, but compared with yesterday I feel a hell of a lot better.'

'Good. Here are your pills. You're down to two at a time now. And,' she added, smiling at him, 'instead of water, I'll make you some tea.'

'Wonderful!' He caught her by the hand. 'What would I have done without you?'

'Made your own tea, I suppose!'

CHAPTER SIX

ONCE James had taken his medication and drunk enough liquid to satisfy her, Eleri folded the blankets she'd slept in and left them in a neat pile on the chest at the foot of the bed.

'Are you going now?' James asked quietly.

'No. But there's no point in trying to sleep again at this hour. Not for me, anyway. You, on the other hand, can do with all the sleep you can get for a while, as a healing process.' Eleri smiled at him cheerfully. 'I'm going next door for a bath, then I shall haul Nico out of bed and raid your fridge to make him some breakfast. I shall bully you into eating something, too.'

He tugged at a forelock. 'Yes, ma'am. And Eleri...' he added as she went to the door.

'Yes?'

'Thank you.'

She smiled and went out of the room, suddenly desperate to remove the clothes she'd slept in and soak in a hot bath for a while. Afterwards, a towel swathed round her damp hair, she opened James's door a crack and found that he was sleeping, just as she'd hoped.

Deciding it was too early to disturb Nico, Eleri

went up to the kitchen, made herself some coffee and toast, and ate it in blissful solitude at James's kitchen table with only Radio Four for company. Later, when Nico arrived in the kitchen ready in the sober uniform of his school, she won his deep approval by presenting him with a plate of bacon and eggs.

'Fab! How's James?' he asked. 'I popped my head round his door just now, but he was sleeping.'

'He's not wonderful, but he's a lot better. The medication's working. His temperature's down this morning.'

'Was he off his head again last night at all?'

'Only once. Nothing I couldn't handle.' Eleri busied herself with pouring coffee to hide her heightened colour.

'Are you staying here today, El? I could come back again tonight, if you like,' he offered eagerly, mouth full.

'I thought you had football practice.'

'I do, but I could come round after that.'

Eleri laughed. 'So you can take advantage of my kind heart and stay up late again, I suppose?'

'No,' he retorted, wounded. 'I just thought I could help, that's all.'

'And you did,' she said warmly. 'I'd never have got James off the floor without you.'

'He's cool,' said Nico casually, downing his coffee. 'I like him.'

'Good. In that case you can go downstairs and see if he's awake.'

While Eleri was clearing away his breakfast Nico came bounding back. 'James is awake, but he doesn't look all that marvellous, El.'

'No. He's only marginally better than yesterday,' she agreed, frowning, and ushered her brother out into the hall. 'Mind how you get that bike out. Are you warm enough in just a blazer?'

'Those are Ma's lines, not yours!' He grinned, wheeled his bicycle outside carefully, punched the air in salute and rode off, leaving Eleri staring after him, hugging her arms across her chest. After a moment she breathed in deeply, shut the door, and went downstairs to ask James what he wanted for breakfast.

'I'm not exactly ravenous, Nurse,' he said warily.

'I don't imagine you are. How about a spoonful of scrambled egg and a finger or two of toast?'

He heaved a deep sigh. 'For you, Miss Conti, anything.'

She smiled slyly. 'Or you could have some devilled kidneys.'

'How you do go on about kidneys,' he said, shuddering. 'Never mention them in my hearing again—devilled or otherwise. Scrambled eggs would be wonderful. And good, strong coffee? I lust for caffeine.'

When Eleri returned with a loaded tray a few minutes later, James pressed her to stay and keep him company while he ate.

'Because I've had an idea,' he said, as he began on his breakfast.

Eleri poured herself some coffee and sat down, looking at him expectantly.

'This is good,' he said appreciatively. 'I'm more hungry than I thought.'

'You ate nothing yesterday,' she reminded him. 'What was this idea?'

'When you were talking about the coffee-shop you worried me, Eleri,' he said, surprising her.

'Really? Why?'

'There was such a trapped, hunted look about you. So I gave it some thought. If I approached your parents personally, told them how much I'd like you back at Northwold, perhaps they'd find it easier to part with you.'

She poured coffee for him and took the empty plate away. 'They might.'

James looked at her over his cup. 'They'd have to part with you one day, anyway. In the natural way of things you're unlikely to work at either the coffee-shop or Northwold for ever.'

She frowned. 'What do you mean?'

'Eleri, you're clever, good-looking, highly efficient and—more of a rarity—compassionate. You proved that beyond all doubt last night by staying here to care for me.' James smiled at her. 'Some lucky guy's bound to sweep you off with him sooner or later—and, hey presto, a home of your own.'

Eleri smiled wryly. 'But I wouldn't be living alone in it.'

'Is that what you want?'

'Yes. Preferably in a flat like this. Unlike you, I've never had a place of my own. Time for your pills,' she added inexorably.

When the ritual was over James looked at her intently. 'You haven't commented on the bit I threw in there, about coming back to Northwold. Change your mind, Eleri. I never really suspected you of leaking information, but placed as we were I was forced to ask. So forgive me. Please. And come back?'

She eyed him curiously. 'But why, James? Surely there must be someone out there who could easily take my place.'

'I want someone who can use her own initiative—someone, moreover, who knows the brewing industry inside out.' He coughed a little, then lay back against the pillows. 'I need someone I can trust to keep things functioning smoothly when I'm away from the office—accompany me sometimes on my travels when an assistant's called for. In short—you, Eleri.'

The prospect of travelling anywhere with James Kincaid was so ravishing it took Eleri's breath away. She sat motionless for a moment, thinking furiously. If she asked them she knew perfectly well her parents would find someone to replace her at the restaurant. In which case it was a bit silly to refuse the Northwold job solely because of her secret feelings for the managing director. After all, she reminded herself, they were nothing new. Nor was the episode last night anything to worry about either. That had been an accident arising from James's delirium, with no danger of any future repetition. If she did go back to Northwold all she had to do was make sure her future relationship with James remained a purely business-like arrangement. Just as it had always been.

'I'll think it over,' she said slowly at last.

James brightened. 'Does that mean you'll discuss it with your family?'

'When the right moment presents itself, yes.'

'How about this evening?'

Eleri smiled. 'Are things so bad back at the office, then?'

'Utter chaos,' he said promptly. 'Which will only get worse if I'm off sick for a while.'

'Which you will be,' she assured him. 'Nico went back to school too soon after his dose of flu and had to take more time off. And he,' she added with cruel emphasis, 'is a supremely fit teenager.'

'You mean a doddering old chap like me needs to be more careful!'

Eleri grinned. 'I wouldn't have put it quite like that, but yes. At least wait until you've finished the antibiotics.'

'If you're willing to stay here and nurse me I'm happy to stay off work indefinitely,' he said promptly, eyes dancing. Then he sobered. 'But seriously, I can manage perfectly well now, Eleri. You look tired. It's time you went home.'

'I thought I'd stay here until after lunch. Then I'll go home, and pop back here for an hour this evening and organise dinner,' she said matter-of-factly. 'You won't need to take any pills through the night, so you can manage on your own after that.'

He nodded morosely. 'I know. But I'll miss my nurse.'

Suddenly Eleri felt irritated. It was all well and good to be praised for her compassion as a nurse and her efficiency as an assistant. But it would be rather nice if James Kincaid simply thought of her as a woman for once—preferably when he was in his right mind, and not hallucinating.

Later that evening Eleri dined with her family before her parents went off, as usual, to the trattoria.

'You look tired, *cara*,' said her father disapprovingly. 'This man Kincaid. Has he no family he can call on to look after him?'

Eleri explained the circumstances. 'I could hardly leave him, Pa. He was very ill last night.'

'Looked terrible,' agreed Nico. 'He's a nice bloke, though, Pop. You'd like him.'

Mario Conti's expression made it plain he doubted that very much. 'Eleri, I trust you are not intending to spend another night with this man?'

She shook her head. 'After this I'm going over there for an hour to give him something to eat, then I'm coming home. Don't worry,' she added rather cuttingly, 'I'll be ready to report for duty in the morning.'

'That's not fair!' said her mother sharply. 'We

weren't worried on that score, and well you know it, my girl.'

'Yes. I do,' said Eleri with contrition. 'I'm sorry.'

'If she does need to stay with James, I can go with her,' offered Nico eagerly.

'James, is it?' said Catrin.

'He *said* to call him that,' said Nico indignantly. 'And I was a help, just as you said.'

'I'm glad to hear it,' she retorted, and eyed Eleri's abandoned meal anxiously. 'Not hungry?'

'No.'

Mario frowned. 'Do you feel ill?'

'No. Just tired.' She turned heavy dark eyes on his face. 'And nervous. I've got something to say, and I'm trying to find the best way to go about it.'

Nico eyed her uneasily. 'Want me to go?'

'No.' She smiled at him, a hint of appeal in her eyes.

He looked at her narrowly for a moment, then returned the smile. 'I wanted more pudding anyway.'

'What is it, Eleri?' her mother asked anxiously. 'Is it something to do with the coffee-shop?'

'Yes.' Eleri breathed in deeply. 'Now please don't be hurt, but this has to be said. I'm just not suited to the coffee-shop. I miss the kind of work I did at Northwold. So I think I'll revert to my original plan and start applying for jobs in London.'

Her father stiffened visibly. 'You mean leave Pennington?'

She nodded. 'I love you all. You know that. But,

unlike Vicky and most of my friends, I've never had a place of my own.' She gave a nervous little chuckle. 'I'm a dinosaur—an anachronism.'

'Time to leave home when you marry!' stated her father flatly.

'Pa, don't be so medieval!' said Eleri in despair.

'You never talked about London jobs when you worked at Northwold,' said Catrin thoughtfully, getting up to collect plates.

'But I used to go to London at weekends.'

'You still can do that, if you give us notice,' interjected her father.

'I know! That's not what I'm talking about.'

'No more now,' advised her mother. 'We'll discuss it later.'

'It won't make any difference,' warned Eleri.

Catrin Conti gave her a quelling look. 'Leave it for now. I've made a pan of *cawl*. You can take it over to Mr Kincaid for his supper, and there's enough to be reheated tomorrow. I expect he can manage to do that for himself.'

'He's a pretty competent sort of man, Mother,' said Eleri tartly. 'Normally I imagine he can manage most things. That's what he is by profession after all— managing director at the Gloucester plant of Northwold.' She bit her lip. 'But thank you, that was a very kind thought. I'm sure he'll appreciate it.'

'More, it seems,' said Mario Conti austerely, 'than you do, Eleri.'

She winced. Her father used her first name only

when he was displeased with her. She never addressed her mother as 'Mother' either, unless they were indulging in one of their rare disagreements.

'I'm very grateful to you both—always. As you well know,' she said quietly. 'Please leave the clearing up. I'll do it.'

'I'll help,' offered Nico, who'd been uncharacteristically quiet during the family argument.

When their parents had left for the trattoria, Nico put his arm around Eleri and gave her a big hug.

'Don't worry, El. It's time Pop was dragged into the twentieth century. It's a miracle you haven't taken off long before now. I'll miss you, though.'

She hugged him back fiercely. 'Thanks, love.'

'I'll see to this,' he said, giving her a push. 'Go on. Take Ma's famous soup over to James. Make sure he's all right.'

Eleri eyed him curiously. 'You really like him, don't you?'

'So do you.' His grin was impish. 'And—don't thump me— I think he quite likes you too.'

'He was grateful to me for staying to look after him, that's all,' she said sedately. 'But I'll take advantage of your kind offer—thank you kindly. I won't be late back home. Pa will be steaming round to Chester Gardens ordering James to make an honest woman of me if I stay another night.'

To Eleri's surprise she found James, dressed in a black roll-neck sweater and jeans, stretched out on the sofa in his study when she let herself into the flat.

'Don't get up!' she ordered as he tried to get to his feet. 'What are you doing out of bed?'

'The doctor called back earlier. He said it was OK as long as I took it easy, because my temperature's normal now,' said James, his voice still hoarse. 'Hello, Eleri,' he added deliberately, 'how nice to see you.'

'Hello, James,' she said with a grin. 'Sorry to come the sergeant major again. How do you feel?'

'Parts of me feel better,' he said cautiously. 'But the legs are a bit rubbery, and I can't get rid of this damn cough.'

'You'll soon be better.'

'I hope so! I thought I'd do some of the work I brought home with me. But I had to call quits on that after a few minutes.'

'Very sensible. How's the appetite? Have you eaten anything since I saw you last?'

He looked guilty. 'I've drunk a lot of orange juice. And,' he added with simple pride, 'I made myself some tea and ate some of those delicious cakes your mother made.'

'Time for some dinner, then,' she said briskly.

'Are you going to share it with me?' he asked hopefully.

'No. I had mine with the family. But my mother made you some *cawl*.'

'That's extraordinarily good of her,' said James, startled. 'What exactly is—what you said?'

'The Welsh version of *pot-au-feu*—bits of lamb

cooked in stock with leeks and loads of other vegetables. Just the ticket for an invalid—nourishing and very good.'

'I'm sure it is.' He looked gloomy. 'I'm causing a lot of trouble for your family, one way and another.'

'I wouldn't say that.' Eleri smiled. 'Though my father wouldn't be thrilled, exactly, if I suggested spending another night here.'

'I would!' James grinned, then eyed her thoughtfully. 'How do you cope with your father's attitude? Forgive me for mentioning a lady's age, but you're no longer a teenager, Eleri.'

'No. In a month's time I'll be thirty, which is a rather sobering thought.' She smiled ruefully. 'I grin and bear it because, to be frank, I've never really met anyone worth making a fuss for.'

'Even Maynard?'

'Good heavens, no.' She shrugged carelessly. 'Toby and I had fun together. But the casual nature of the relationship was the most appealing thing about it. I saw him only occasionally, when I went up to London. My parents weren't worried. They know that emotional involvement isn't on my agenda. How did we get on to all this?' she added abruptly, shaking her head. 'Not a subject for an empty stomach. I'm off to heat the soup.'

James had no dining room, and Eleri, fairly sure he was by no means feeling as well as he made out, insisted he ate from a tray in the study rather than in the kitchen as he'd suggested.

When she laid the tray across his knees James sniffed appreciatively.

'This smells wonderful, Eleri. Are you sure you won't have some?'

'No, thanks.' She curled up in a corner of the sofa beside him, nursing a mug of coffee. 'Over family dinner the subject of my desertion of the coffee-shop acted as a pretty efficient appetite depressant.'

'How did it go down?'

'Where my father was concerned like a lead balloon.'

'So what will you do?'

Eleri looked at the bulging briefcase, at the familiar welter of paperwork on the desk. Her eyes went to the computer and the fax machine, and she felt a sudden, fierce urge to get back to the work she was trained for. 'Is the offer of the job still open?' she asked abruptly.

James put down his spoon very carefully. 'It's never been closed.'

'In that case I'll come back, if you'll have me,' she said without drama.

'You know damn well I will!'

'Thank you.' Eleri thought for a moment. 'I'll stay where I am until my father's organised a replacement manager. But in the evenings, while you're convalescing, I can come round and help you with this lot— and anything else Northwold sends out to you.'

He looked at her searchingly. 'Does this mean I'm

forgiven for daring to question you about the take-over?'

'Not quite.' Eleri gave him a tight little smile. 'Let's say I'm willing to overlook it.'

'Very noble of you,' said James dryly, picking up his spoon again. 'So, Miss Conti. Next Monday I'll expect you back at Northwold.'

'You're not getting back there yourself before then, I hope?' she said quickly. 'You may be better, but you're not feeling all that wonderful—admit it!'

'I do,' he said with a sigh, then grinned at her. 'But with the prospect of having my paragon back—aided by a bowlful or two of your mother's miraculous pick-me-up—I'll soon be fit. Small wonder young Nico's fit if he takes this in regular doses.'

'He likes you,' Eleri informed him.

'I like him too. Bring him round again when I'm back to normal '

'It's suddenly occurred to me,' she said thought-fully. 'It's a good thing the party was cancelled if it was supposed to be a send-off for me—' She stopped at the wry look on James's face.

'Actually, it wasn't,' he admitted. 'It was intended as a means of tempting you back.'

'So you invited me on false pretences.'

'With the best of intentions,' he assured her, be-ginning to cough.

Eleri jumped up and rescued the remains of his dinner, eyeing him with concern. 'I assume you take the next lot of pills at nine-fifteen?'

James nodded speechlessly. She handed him a glass of mineral water and he drank gratefully, then sat back, panting. 'Damn cough. Though I don't do it so often now. And,' he added, 'the pills are the last lot for today.'

'Make sure you finish the entire course,' she instructed as she took the tray.

'Yes, Nurse,' he said mockingly.

'People who are rarely ill are rarely sensible about medication either,' she said severely, and smiled. 'I speak from experience with Nico. I had to get quite tough with him more than once.'

'I can picture it clearly,' said James with feeling, and eyed her cajolingly. 'Do you have to rush off now?'

'No. I can stay for a while if you like.' Eleri cast a longing look at the cluttered desk. 'Would you like me to make a start—?'

'Don't even think of it,' he said flatly. 'Just sit down and talk to me for a while. I've missed you.'

Eleri resumed her place next to him. 'That's because you're under the weather.' She smiled wryly. 'I confess that at one stage in the night, when you were delirious again, I cursed myself for not hiring a nurse from one of the agencies.'

'For influenza?' he said scornfully, then frowned. 'But you're right. That's exactly what you should have done. I was an idiot not to think of it.'

'I didn't mind looking after you,' she said hastily.

'I was just worried you needed more professional attention than mine.'

'No one could have done better,' James assured her, then paused for a moment, eyeing her. 'If you meant what you said about coming here tomorrow night—'

'I always mean what I say.'

'Good. Then could you arrange some dinner for us from your father's restaurant, and bring it round to share it with me?' He fished in his back pocket for his wallet and held out some money. 'Choose whatever you want.'

Eleri was about to refuse indignantly, then it occurred to her that it might be best to keep everything on a business footing. She got up and took the notes. 'All right, I will. There's enough of my mother's soup to reheat for your lunch. What about shopping?'

'My cleaner's due in the morning. I'll give her a list.'

'Right. I'll just clear away your meal, then I'll be off.' Eleri grimaced. 'My mother wants a talk with me, so I'd better not stay away too long. What would you like me to bring for the meal?'

James got up. 'Anything you fancy. I'll take the tray for you.'

'No, you won't.' Eleri bore it away before he could reach it, but James followed her into the kitchen and sat at the table, watching her.

When she'd finished James rose to his feet to bar her way as she made for the door. He took her by the elbows, smiling down at her. 'George Reeder told me you were heaven-sent, but he didn't know the half of it.'

Eleri stood very still, feeling the imprint of his fingers through the wool of her sweater. 'I'm glad to help.' She looked up, transfixed for a moment by the look of undisguised desire in his eyes, then turned her head sharply as he bent to kiss her. His lips touched her cheek lingeringly, then he released her, smiling crookedly, and walked with her to the door.

'A mere token of my appreciation, Eleri.'

She searched in her bag to hide her heightened colour, and handed his key to him.

'Keep it, please,' he said quickly. 'I might have a relapse.'

'After all my efforts, don't you dare,' she said tartly. 'Goodnight. Don't forget your pills, and try to get a good night's sleep. And keep your liquid intake up and remember to eat lunch tomorrow.

All the way home in the car Eleri's cheek burned from the touch of James's mouth as her words echoed in her ears—brusque, bossy and not at all the way to speak to a man she hoped to work for again. But the kiss had shaken her, and her trenchant little departing lecture had been a cover for her own instinctive response to it. Ill or not, James had, at that particular moment at least, wanted her. In which case, said an intrusive voice in her mind, returning to work for him was hardly the sensible thing to do.

So? she retorted fiercely. All her adult life she'd

made a positive religion of being sensible, as penance for one solitary, almost-forgotten lapse from grace. Eleri knew very well she was thought of as the clever, level-headed Conti daughter. And there were times when living up to the description was not only difficult, but a dead bore.

CHAPTER SEVEN

CATRIN CONTI was alone in the sitting room, watching a newscast on television, a teatray on a small table beside her. She looked up with a smile as her daughter came into the room. 'Hello, *cariad*. How's Mr Kincaid?'

'Better. He sent his thanks for the *cawl*. I just waited to clear away after he'd eaten, then I came back.' Eleri eyed her mother warily, then sat down. 'Busy in the restaurant tonight?'

'The usual Monday night crowd.' Catrin switched off the television. 'They don't need me, so I thought I'd have a cup of tea in peace.'

The lull before the storm, thought Eleri, and took the war into the enemy's camp. 'I hope you weren't terribly upset earlier.'

'No. I'm not blind, Eleri. I know your heart isn't in running the coffee-shop.' Catrin shrugged. 'You've been trained for very different work. It's only natural you want to return to the kind of thing you do best.'

'So you don't mind?' said Eleri, astonished.

Her mother chuckled. 'In one way I do, of course. But I can appreciate your point of view.'

'Does Papa?'

'Your father comes from a different culture, love.

110

You can't expect him to feel happy about his daughter wanting to take off to London. Especially you, *cariad*.'

'Especially me,' agreed Eleri bitterly. 'But it's what I always intended, Ma.'

'I know. I've had a talk with your father and I've convinced him that binding you too close might achieve just the opposite.'

'Have you now?' Eleri eyed her mother with respect. 'I really did my best to make a go of it at the coffee-shop.'

'And a very good best it is, too.' Catrin eyed her daughter speculatively. 'Will you carry on there for us, please, until your father arranges someone else to take over?'

'Yes, of course.'

'Don't worry—you can have time off now and again to look for another job.'

'I won't need it.' Eleri looked her mother in the eye. 'James Kincaid's asked me again to go back to Northwold. And this time I said yes. You don't look surprised,' she added.

'I'm not, really. Ever since you went out that night with him I've been expecting it, in a way. And I can't help feeling relieved.' Catrin smiled. 'Your father will be too. You were a clever madam, Eleri Conti, threatening him with London. You meant to go back to Northwold all the time!'

Eleri smiled smugly. 'Mr Kincaid was very persuasive.'

'Why, I wonder?'

Eleri shrugged. 'Apparently he hasn't been able to find anyone suitable to take my place. But I won't start back until you find someone for the coffee-shop.'

'I can take that over myself as a temporary measure.'

'No way,' said Eleri emphatically. 'In that case I'll tell Mr Kincaid I've changed my mind. If Papa finds another manager I'll go back to Northwold. If not I'll stay.'

'All right, *cariad*. When your father comes back I'll see what I can do.'

Given a clear picture of the alternative by his wife, Mario Conti bestowed his blessing on Eleri's desire to return to Northwold. A new waitress was engaged for the coffee-shop, a delighted Gianni would take over the management role, and Catrin let her husband believe that it was his own idea that she herself resume responsibility for the daily ordering for both café and restaurant.

'My mother's so clever,' confided Eleri to James, when she'd switched off the computer the following evening. 'She manages to run the entire household and restaurant as the sort of power behind my father's throne.'

'How did she manage when she was producing babies?' he asked with interest.

'My grandmother used to come up from Cardiff, and my Italian grandparents would come over from

Italy.' She turned away and began putting a sheaf of papers in order. 'When Nico was born my sister and I lent a hand as well. Nico goes wild if I mention it, but I could change a nappy very efficiently right from the start.'

'I believe you.' James's dark-ringed eyes were intent on her averted face. 'Will you ever get as close to a man as you are to Nico, I wonder?' he said thoughtfully. 'If you do he'll be a lucky guy. Efficiency's your middle name.'

'Actually, it's Caterina,' she said tartly, clipping the last batch of papers together. 'Shall I make some coffee? I must go soon.'

He got up hastily, looking remorseful. 'I'll make it. You've done enough.'

'No need,' she said crisply 'Sit down—please. You're still a bit white around the gills when you get up suddenly, James.'

When she got back he eyed her searchingly as she laid the tray on the desk.

She smiled brightly. 'Black or white?'

'Black.' He took the cup from her, his eyes bright with comprehension. 'Can it be that you tire, sometimes, of praise for your efficiency?'

'I don't tire of the praise!'

'Only the efficiency tag.'

'Yes. Silly, really.'

'Not at all.' His eyes softened. 'There's a great more to you in every way than mere efficiency. You look tired,' he added, frowning. 'Hell, I hope you're not coming down with flu, Eleri.'

'Because you want me back at my desk next Monday?'

'No, dammit! Because I'll feel directly responsible if you get ill—and guilty as hell for letting you stay here to look after me.'

Eleri refilled their coffee-cups and sat down beside him. 'You didn't let me do anything. It was my decision to stay,' she said very deliberately. 'And I don't feel ill, but I do feel tired. I've been on my feet all day, and I've put in an hour's work here tonight. Something,' she added, 'my parents don't know, by the way. They think I was coming here just to bring your dinner and see how you are.'

'Which is all you should have done,' he said morosely.

'James, I was glad to do some work. I've missed it. Besides, it was only a few faxes.'

'It was a damn sight more than that!' He took her hand. 'You don't know how relieved I feel at the prospect of having you back at Northwold. I've missed you like hell.'

Eleri's heart thumped as she looked down at their clasped hands, knowing she should pull away, but liking the feel of his long fingers entwined with her own. 'You were used to me, that's all.'

He reached up the other hand to turn her face to his, and their eyes met. 'You mean I took you for granted.'

Eleri didn't trouble to deny it, because his nearness was affecting her so badly she was afraid to trust her voice. James's eyes fell to the sudden, hurried rise and fall of her breasts beneath her red silk shirt, and with a smothered groan he pulled her into his arms and kissed her hungrily, giving her no time to fight back the response which ran through her like a tidal wave, as all-consuming as before. She gasped, her lips parting to kisses which quickly grew fevered, and he hauled her onto his lap and held her so tightly she couldn't move. Not that she wanted to. Eleri would have been happy to stay where she was indefinitely, returning his kisses with fervour, but soon she felt his deft, practised fingers begin to undo her shirt and she stiffened. He locked both arms around her and stifled her wordless protest with a kiss which left them breathless and shaking when he raised his head, his eyes glittering with urgency.

'Come to bed,' he whispered, and for the second time in as many days Eleri came back to earth with a bump.

She pushed him away and shot to her feet, her face averted, tidying herself with unsteady hands as she listened to the slowing rasp of James's breathing.

'Eleri,' he said gruffly at last. 'Look at me.'

She turned reluctantly, and he raked a hand through his hair, eyeing her warily. 'What can I say? I didn't mean that to happen.'

'Let's forget it ever did,' she said tightly, her eyes stormy. 'It's my fault. I should have left you to get on with your flu as best you could. I obviously sent out the wrong signals.'

He caught one of her hands in his, tightening it when she tried to pull it away. 'No. You didn't. You took care of me because you're warm and compassionate. I was a stupid fool to take advantage of it.' He smiled wryly. 'Don't blame me too much, Eleri. You don't seem to know just how desirable you are— I'm only human.'

Eleri detached her hand and put on her coat quickly, before he had the chance to hold it for her. He wasn't entirely to blame, she knew. If she'd frozen him off at once the incident would have been all over before it started. 'As I said before,' she said tightly, 'let's forget it.'

'Easier said than done.' James stood very erect, his mouth set as he looked down at her. 'Does this mean you'll change your mind about coming back to work with me?'

Eleri regarded him analytically for a moment or two. 'No. I'm not high-minded enough to give up a job I like over a—a trivial incident like this.'

James's eyes narrowed dangerously for a moment. He breathed in deeply. 'Right. Then you'll start back next Monday?'

'Yes.' Fatigue suddenly overwhelmed her. 'Goodnight.'

'You're exhausted,' he said grimly. 'Eleri—' He stopped short, shrugging impatiently. 'Whatever I say at this point will only make things worse. So goodnight, Eleri. Drive carefully.'

Far from feeling angry with James over his lovemaking, Eleri felt rather pleased with life as she drove home, apart from a slight headache. When she got to the house she made hot drinks for herself and Nico, then told him she was off to bed early for once with a book, eager to get there before her parents came home.

He eyed her narrowly. 'You look a bit seedy, El.'

'I'm just tired. I need some sleep. And you do too, by the way. Don't be long.'

Upstairs Eleri swallowed a couple of painkillers, drank her hot milk, then climbed into bed to surrender to thoughts of James's kisses and the feelings he'd aroused in her. She'd wanted James to make love to her—so badly, in fact, that she'd almost given in—but not in such a casual way, arising out of the sheer propinquity of the past few days. If—when—she took a lover for real, she would require some romance about it: flowers and music, protestations of love over a candlelit dinner, even. And why not? It was no more than a clever, efficient, and—according to James—desirable female like herself deserved. One, moreover, who was going back to independence and the job she loved. Eleri fell asleep smiling, only to wake in the small hours with a fit of sneezing. By next morning it was painfully obvious that she was unfit to serve the public.

'I knew it,' raged her father. 'You wear yourself out looking after this man Kincaid, and now you are ill too.'

'I've got a cold, Pa,' she said thickly. 'Half the population of Pennington's got a cold. And quite a lot of them come into the coffee-shop.'

'Straight back to bed,' ordered her mother.

'But I haven't got flu,' protested Eleri.

'No. You've got a messy old cold. And if you stay in bed today you'll get rid of it all the faster,' said Catrin firmly. 'I'll go over the road to do the ordering, then I'll pop up to see you. Your father can supervise Gianni today.'

Eleri acquiesced gratefully, filled a hot water bottle, made herself a mug of tea, commandeered the mobile phone and went back upstairs to enjoy the unexpected pleasure of being tucked up in a warm bed instead of ministering to the public in the coffee-shop. Halfway through the morning the phone rang.

'Eleri?' said James. 'They told me at the coffee-shop you were ill. What's the matter? You've caught my bug, of course. I knew this would happen!'

'I've got a cold,' she contradicted him. 'A messy, unsightly cold in the head. Not flu.'

'Are you in bed?'

'Yes. Complete with hot water bottle, radio and gruesome thriller.'

'Ah. Enjoying ill health?'

'Right.'

He coughed a little, the cause embarrassment, she

decided, rather than respiratory. 'I rang to apologise again for last night.'

'No need,' she assured him airily. 'I've forgotten all about it.'

'How fortunate for you,' he snapped. 'And in case you're worried about my eating arrangements this evening, Camilla's coming down from London.'

Eleri scowled, unseen. 'I wasn't. Worried, I mean. But I'm glad you're being taken care of.'

'Thank you,' he said distantly. 'I hope you feel better soon.'

'It's only a cold. I'll be fit by Monday.'

'That's not what I meant.'

Eleri interrupted him with a huge, explosive sneeze, which gave her the excuse to bid him a swift goodbye. So. Camilla was back on the scene. Eleri couldn't help hoping James was still contagious. She spent a pleasant moment or two visualising a feverish, germ-laden Camilla with lank hair and hollow eyes, then gave herself a stringent lecture on her lack of charity, reminding herself that when she faced James across his desk next Monday, both of them would revert automatically to their right and proper places. And stay in them.

Eleri decided she deserved the luxury of an entire day in bed, warning her family to steer clear. Catrin chose to ignore this at lunchtime, declaring that her daughter needed nourishment.

'Feed a cold and starve a fever,' she said firmly, and put a tray over Eleri's knees. '*Zuppa di funghi—*

only I had to make the soup with tame mushrooms, not wild ones. I've grated a bit of cheese on top.'

'Thank you,' said Eleri appreciatively. 'I'm starving. Don't come too near.'

Catrin retreated to the door obediently. 'Were you supposed to go round to Mr Kincaid tonight?'

Eleri shook her head. 'No. I'm not seeing him until next Monday at Northwold.'

'Just as well, looking like that. Anything else you fancy, love?'

'No, thanks, this is fine. Don't come up again. I'll have a little nap after lunch.'

Eleri got up next day, no longer sneezing, but grateful when she was ordered to stay at home and take care of herself.

Mid-morning, James rang again. 'How are you, Eleri?'

'Better, thanks. And you?'

'Almost back to normal. Boredom is my main complaint at the moment.'

Boredom? With the fair Camilla on hand?

'I rang to make sure you weren't intending to come round tonight,' he went on.

'I wasn't,' she assured him breezily. Did the man think he could alternate her with Camilla?

'I meant,' said James harshly, 'that much as I would like to see you tonight I'd rather you took care of yourself and got well quickly.'

'It's very kind of you to be so concerned. Thank

you. By the way, do they know at Northwold that I'm coming back, or should I be notifying anyone?'

'I've told Bruce to inform Personnel. He was very pleased, by the way.'

'How nice of him. I'll see you next Monday at the plant, then.'

'Not before?' he said sharply.

'No, James. The last thing you need is my cold. Take care of yourself. Bye.'

Eleri put down the phone, feeling rather pleased with herself. She felt even more so at lunchtime, when an exquisite hand-tied bouquet of spring flowers arrived for her, with a simple message of thanks from James.

'Goodness, they're lovely!' said her mother. 'What a nice thought.' She glanced at her daughter narrowly. 'You look rather smug, *cariad*.'

Eleri grinned. 'I don't get bouquets of flowers every day of the week.'

'If your cold's better by the weekend why not go up to stay with Vicky for a day or two?'

'Can't. She's off to the sun on Saturday. Don't worry, Ma. I'll be fine.'

Catrin smoothed her daughter's hair with a gentle hand. 'I know you will. But no coming back to the coffee-shop. Have a little break before you go back to Northwold.'

When Eleri parked her car in her usual place at Northwold the following Monday, it was as though she'd never been away—but with one slight difference. She timed her arrival to coincide with the rest of the office staff. As she'd hoped, Bruce Gordon and a couple of the other managers were in with James when she passed his door. She was greeted with a general chorus of welcome from all four men, and resumed her place at her desk a little later with a pleasurable feeling of homecoming.

The other female members of staff in the administration block had all expressed their pleasure in her return, she had completely recovered from her cold, and she was wearing her favourite black suit. When James buzzed for her at last, Eleri felt reasonably composed, despite the familiar, hard scrutiny trained on her as she approached his desk. He rose, looking a little drawn and dark under the eyes, but otherwise much the same as usual.

'Good morning, Eleri, welcome back,' he said crisply. 'You look well, so I take it you're fully recovered.'

'Yes, thank you, Mr Kincaid.' She smiled pleasantly. 'How are *you* feeling?'

'Not exactly one hundred percent yet, but I'm getting there. You were late this morning,' he added.

'No. Not late. I merely arrived at the same time as the others.'

His jaw tightened. 'To avoid being alone with me?'

'It seemed best.' She looked at him enquiringly. 'Are you ready to start work now, or would you like some coffee first?'

'Bring your chair over, please, Eleri. Before we start work there are one or two things I want to say.'

She sat down in her usual place, but James put his hands on the desk and leaned forward, his eyes boring into hers.

'When you left so precipitately, we had worked together for twelve months—'

'Thirteen, actually.'

'Right. In that time we established a reasonable working relationship. Do you agree?'

Eleri nodded. 'Yes.'

'But since then we've come to know each other rather better.' His eyes gleamed coldly. 'And by your attitude it's obvious you think I'll take advantage of the fact.'

'Of course I don't,' said Eleri, her face pink. 'It was the other way round.'

James sat down, frowning. 'You actually thought I'd suspect *you* of getting too familiar? Is that why I'm Mr Kincaid again, instead of James?'

'You're the MD. I'm your assistant. The formality is necessary,' she said firmly.

'Eleri,' he said, his voice ultra-dry, 'just because I stepped out of line once doesn't mean I'm likely to take advantage of the fact now I've managed to get you back to work for me. I wouldn't dare in case you walked out again.'

She smiled involuntarily, and James nodded in approval.

'That's better. Thank you for your note.'

'Thank *you* for the flowers.'

'I would have preferred a telephone call.'

'I was brought up to write thank-you letters,' she said lightly, and cast a meaningful eye over the pile of paperwork on his desk.

'All right, all right,' he said irritably. 'Let's make a start.'

The brief exchange cleared the air to a certain extent; Eleri was satisfied that certain lines had been drawn. Lines she had no intention of crossing over to return to the unintentional intimacy created by James's illness. While he was briefly dependent on her he'd begun to look on her as more than just a paragon of efficiency. Which was dangerous. A relationship with James Kincaid was out of the question for several reasons, not least because she cared for him too much. With James it would be all or nothing, not the uninvolving type of friendship she had enjoyed with Toby.

After the first few days back at Northwold, Eleri not only felt as though she'd never been away but that the interlude at Chester Gardens had never occurred. Which, she conceded, was entirely her own fault. James had made it plain he would have preferred things on a less formal footing once they were back at Northwold together. To avoid this Eleri kept to a purely professional attitude. And by the end of the first week, after a few false starts on James's part, the arrangement was working well. Exactly as she wanted. So why, she asked herself irritably, didn't she feel happier about it?

Eleri had been back at Northwold for three weeks when her father asked if she would lend a hand in the trattoria one Saturday night.

'Not to wait on tables, *cara*, but if you would take the money and see to the drinks it would help. Luigi is on holiday and Dario's ill. Your mother and I are needed in the kitchen.'

'Of course I'll help.'

By seven that evening Eleri was behind the little bar in the trattoria, wearing the black jersey tunic and skirt she'd worn to dinner with James, heavy gold rings in her ears, and her hair caught back at one side with a black velvet clasp. Saturday nights were always busy, and from the first she was kept fully occupied.

The rush had reached its climax, and begun to subside a little, when a new pair of arrivals came to the bar. Eleri looked up with a smile which congealed abruptly at the sight of James Kincaid. With companion.

'Good evening, Eleri,' said James, his eyes gleaming. 'I know it's a bit late, but would you have a table for two?'

'Good evening,' she said mechanically, fighting to keep her smile in place. James's dinner guest was a very pretty redhead she'd never seen before. Not even Camilla, she thought savagely, and came out from behind the bar to direct James and his companion to the corner table which looked out on the floodlit beauty of St Mark's church by night.

As they seated themselves Eleri handed out two large menus and asked their requirements for drinks.

James waved a hand. 'Venetia Dawson, Eleri Conti. Eleri's my personal assistant at Northwold,' he added to his companion.

'Really!' said the girl, astonished. 'You work *here* as well?'

'Normally, no. My father owns the trattoria,' said Eleri. 'We're suffering from staff shortages tonight, so I'm lending a hand.'

'For which I'm sure your father's very grateful. Eleri's alarmingly efficient at everything she does,' added James to his partner, poker-faced. 'Sometimes I think she's after my job at Northwold.'

The girl laughed. 'And why not, James?'

Why not, indeed? thought Eleri, and smiled serenely. 'If you'll tell me what you'd like in the way of drinks I'll have someone bring them over.'

'A glass of white wine and a Scotch and soda,' said James, and looked up into Eleri's face. 'Do have one yourself,' he said softly.

'I won't, thanks, not while I'm on duty.' She went back to the bar with murder in her heart. She poured the drinks, summoned one of the waiters and handed them over to him, then turned to a customer waiting to pay. 'Sorry to keep you waiting, sir,' she said, with such a radiant smile the man assured her he was in no hurry at all.

Fate was unkind, she thought bitterly as the evening wore on. James must have come out on spec for a meal, seen her at the bar in the trattoria and decided to parade his new girlfriend in front of her. There were eating places enough in Pennington without coming to the Trattoria Veneto, damn the man.

The restaurant was nearly empty by the time James and his companion got up to leave. While the lady went along to the cloakroom James presented the bill and a credit card to Eleri at the bar.

'It was a splendid meal. My compliments to the chef,' he said, smiling, as she put the card through.

'I'll tell my father. He'll be gratified.'

James looked slightly discomfited. 'I thought he'd retired from actual cooking these days.'

'He has, but two of our chefs are off, so my parents pitched in tonight.' Eleri smiled as she handed him a pen to sign the credit card slip. 'I only hope they're on speaking terms by this time.' Her eyes slid past him as Venetia came into view. 'Thank you so much for your patronage,' she said deliberately. 'Goodnight.'

'Goodnight, Eleri. See you on Monday.'

When the restaurant was closed Eleri went back to the house while her parents finished up.

'Oh, boy,' said Nico, tearing himself away from *Match of the Day*. 'Was it that bad?'

'No. I don't mind lending a hand.'

'So what's up?'

'James Kincaid came in for a meal.'

Nico eyed her warily. 'On his own?'

'No. With a drop-dead gorgeous redhead—stop laughing or I'll hit you!'

He threw up his hands, guffawing, then sobered. 'He fancies you rotten, just the same, El.' He patted his nose with a forefinger. 'Men know these things.'

'Oh, do they?' Eleri grinned. 'Right. Bedtime for both of us, Niccolo Conti.'

But when Nico's athletic figure had taken the stairs, two at a time, Eleri remained downstairs, feeling decidedly out of sorts. The cute redhead was to blame, of course. Camilla was one thing—part of James's life before his arrival at Northwold, someone Eleri had known about and accepted all along. But the advent of another woman in his life was hard to swallow.

If she'd known the affair with Camilla was over she might not have insisted on keeping James at arms' length. Too late now. Besides, she thought, eyes flashing, he was a callous swine to parade his new lady-love under her nose at the trattoria. Probably it was his way of paying her back for refusing to let him make love to her. Nevertheless she felt hurt, and desperately disappointed. She had thought James above pettiness of that kind. It was her fault for putting him up on a pedestal. Idols had a tendency to clay feet. James, it seemed, was no exception.

CHAPTER EIGHT

THE following Monday it took Eleri all the self-control she possessed to greet James with the pleasant, impersonal courtesy she'd developed since her return to Northwold. And even for a Monday it was far and away one of the less happy days she'd spent in the job, not least because James was obviously aware of—and amused by—the effort it took for her to be civil.

Due to pressure of work, plus a certain lack of concentration at times, Eleri went on working later than usual. After she'd finally switched off her computer she looked up to find James leaning in the doorway linking their offices.

'Time you knocked off, Eleri.'

'I was just about to.' She got to her feet. 'By the way, would it be possible for me to leave a little earlier on Friday? I'm going away for the weekend.'

'Of course. Take off after lunch, if you like.' He moved towards her. 'You look tired. You could have left all that for the morning.'

'I prefer to leave as little as possible,' she said politely. 'And mid-afternoon on Friday will be soon enough, thank you.'

James raised a quizzical eyebrow. 'Something wrong, Eleri?'

She looked carefully blank. 'No. Nothing. Goodnight.'

'Wait a moment.' He barred her way. 'If something's bothering you I'd like to know.'

Eleri stared doggedly at the knot of his tie. 'I'm fine.' She raised her wrist and looked pointedly at her watch. 'It's late. I must get home.'

With narrowed eyes James stood aside. 'Right. Goodnight, then, Eleri. I'll see you in the morning.'

She nodded pleasantly, and left the office before he thought up any more questions. Tomorrow she would be more careful. She could hardly tell James Kincaid that the 'something wrong' was the flame-haired Venetia. It was odd, really, Eleri reflected as she drove home. When James had first arrived at Northwold she had fully expected such an attractive man to be involved with a woman in some way or another, if not actually married. She had accepted Camilla's part in his life with resignation. But his replacing Camilla with the younger—and more sexy—Venetia touched Eleri on the raw. And the sheer illogicality of her own resentment angered her all the more.

Eleri was calmer by the time she got home. Who was she kidding? James liked her, and had missed her at Northwold, and for a few moments one evening had found her physically appealing. But that was all. Anything more was in her own imagination. And even if it weren't, and James did want her for a more personal reason, there were personal reasons of her own which made it impossible, much as she longed to confide in him. Something which had never happened before. Her heart missed a beat. This, of course, was the problem. James was the first man she'd ever loved. And ever would love. If only... She breathed in deeply. Regrets were pointless. And the half a loaf of their working relationship was better than no contact with James at all.

Next morning Eleri was her usual self again, able to smile at James and mean it when they met first thing.

'You're better,' he said instantly.

'Yes. Sorry about yesterday. I was a bit off-colour.' She took her usual seat and looked across at him expectantly, waiting for him to dive into the paperwork in front of him.

'Where are you going on Friday?' asked James, surprising her.

'London for the weekend.'

'I'm driving up there myself on Friday afternoon. I'll give you a lift.'

Eleri bit her lip, her face suddenly warm. 'I couldn't possibly put you to the trouble—'

'No trouble, Eleri. I'll drop you wherever you want.'

'Thank you. You're very kind,' she responded, hiding her pleasure at the idea by looking pointedly at the pile of work in front of him.

James's smile widened. 'I'm not kind at all. I'd appreciate the company.'

But behind the driving force image he *was* kind, thought Eleri later, as she worked steadily through the morning. Otherwise he wouldn't have troubled to keep her job open when she walked out on him. He'd known how much she loved her job, and he liked her too. He'd never made any secret of that. Of course he hadn't lost by taking her back, because she was good at what she did, but there were any number of women just as good who could have replaced her. So, Venetia or not, she had cause to be grateful to James Kincaid.

The week went by quickly in preparation for the launch of a new type of lager, and Eleri sailed through it all with ease, buoyed up by the thought of her first weekend away since her run-in with Toby. On her way home on Thursday evening she called in on the hairdresser who, from time to time, trimmed off an inch or so of hair and tidied up the shape.

'That looks nice,' said her mother when Eleri got home. 'Does Vicky have any plans for the weekend?'

'No idea. I don't mind what we do.'

'Just good to get away,' nodded Catrin sympathetically. 'Call Nico down, would you, *cariad*? He's supposed to be doing his homework up there. Make sure he finishes it! Your dinner's ready. We've had ours—your father's already gone over to the restaurant and I promised I wouldn't be long. Fully booked tonight.'

'Good. You carry on.' Eleri smiled at her mother. 'I'll see to Nico.'

Eleri enjoyed an evening alone with Nico, despite his constant discourse on the form of Inter Milan and Juventus, and sometimes Liverpool and Manchester United. Eleri listened with attention as she served him two helpings of her mother's famous chicken and ham pie, doing her best to take an interest in the ruling passion of his life.

'Sorry, El,' he said eventually. 'I must be boring you rigid.'

'Me? Bored by football?' she said, widening mocking eyes at him.

He grinned. 'All right. Your turn now. How's James?'

'He's fine. In fact he's driving me to London tomorrow afternoon.'

Nico's eyebrows shot up. 'You're going away with *him*? I thought you were going to Vicky's.'

'I am. He's just giving me a lift.' Eleri eyed him curiously. 'Would you object, then, if I *were* going off with him?'

He shook his head vigorously, and accepted a bowl of chocolate trifle with enthusiasm. 'No way. James is cool. And it's about time you had a real boyfriend, if you ask me.'

'Well, I'm not asking you. And I've had plenty of boyfriends in the past.'

'I know, I know. Not like James, though.'

Which was true enough, thought Eleri as she went

off to bed later. Nico's attitude was surprising. He obviously liked James a lot. And seemed worried because she led such a quiet life. Nor was he the only one. She knew perfectly well her mother felt the same, though her father, she suspected, would have kept her home for ever, given the choice.

Mario Conti drove his daughter to Northwold the next morning since James was giving her a lift to London.

'How will you get back, *cara*?' he asked as she kissed him goodbye.

'By train on Sunday evening. I'll ring you beforehand.'

The morning flew by in Eleri's efforts to get as much done as possible before she left, and shortly after lunch James put his head round the door.

'I'm going down to the car in a few minutes. I'll wait there for you. Don't be long.'

Eleri tidied her desk, then went off to the cloakroom to replace her neat grey suit with black wool trousers and yellow sweater, pulled on her jacket and hurried off with her hold-all to a chorus of well wishes from her colleagues. She was lucky, thought Eleri, to work with people who all seemed genuinely pleased to have her back—if only, they teased, because it meant bidding farewell to the formidable, navy-clad Mrs Willis.

The afternoon was bright, but bitingly cold as the barrier was raised at the gate for James to drive his car away from Northwold property.

'Are you warm enough, Eleri?' he asked.

'Perfectly, thanks.'

'When are you coming back? Sunday?'

'Yes.'

They talked shop, principally about the new launch, as they drove through undulating Gloucestershire countryside. But when they were finally cruising along the motorway in the fast lane he gave her a swift, sideways glance.

'What are your plans for the weekend, Eleri? Nightclub? Theatre?'

'No idea.' Eleri shrugged, smiling. 'Vicky usually has something laid on. We'll probably go to the cinema at some stage. She likes romantic weepies; I like thrillers. So we generally go to one of those multi-screen places and see both.'

'I haven't been to the cinema in years.'

'The Regal in Pennington's very good. I often go there.'

'Alone?'

'Yes. Or with Nico, sometimes, if he's at a loose end.'

His eyes narrowed. 'It never ceases to amaze me that someone with your looks isn't beating off male escorts with a stick.'

Eleri chuckled. 'Is it so difficult to believe I just enjoy my own company?'

'No, because I enjoy it myself. And not only your company,' he added deliberately, 'as I demonstrated so rashly one night. Something I've been kicking my-self for ever since.'

'You don't have to,' she said, her face warm. 'You've already apologised.'

'Ah, but I think I should make it clear that my apology was not for making love to you. How could I be sorry for that? My regret is for my lack of tim-ing.'

Eleri turned to glare at him. 'You think some other time I would have been more co-operative?'

'I didn't mean that,' he snapped.

'Whatever you meant, I'd rather we dropped the subject.'

James inclined his head coldly and drove on with-out a word while Eleri stared stonily at the traffic which clogged three lanes of the motorway as far as the eye could see. They were nearing their destination before James broke the silence to ask Vicky's address.

'No need,' said Eleri stiffly. 'Just drop me at an Underground station wherever convenient.'

'I shall do nothing of the kind. Tell me where your friend lives, please.'

Having learned that Vicky lived in a block of flats not far from Ealing Broadway, James turned off the motorway shortly afterwards and a few minutes later parked outside the building Eleri indicated. James killed the engine and turned to her.

'Eleri, once and for all, I'm not sorry I made love to you, only that I was idiot enough to rush my fences.'

Eleri kept her eyes on the seat belt she was unfastening. 'As I've said before, it doesn't matter. Let's forget about it.'

'But you're still angry,' he said bleakly.

Only about Venetia, you stupid idiot, she wanted to scream at him. Instead she gave him a polite little smile, thanked him for the lift, and opened her door. James got out and came round the car to hand her suitcase over.

'I'll come and pick you up on Sunday.'

Eleri stared, taken aback. 'Oh, but—'

'No buts. I'll be here about four.' And without waiting for an answer James got in the car and drove off without a backward glance.

Victoria Mantle was the same age as Eleri, but there any similarity ended. She was tall, chestnut-haired, opulently curved, and rarely without one man in tow, if not more. She also had a shrewd, mathematical brain, and a hard outer shell that made her a successful trader. But beneath the shell, known only to the favoured few allowed access to it, lay a warm, generous nature and a tigerish tendency to protect those she loved. The moment Vicky answered her doorbell Eleri was swept into a warm embrace, given the choice of coffee, wine or something stronger, and because Eleri was well known for being uncommunicative on the phone, commanded to fill in every detail of what had happened since they last met, including news of Toby, who Vicky described with several four-letter words, none of which would have found favour with Catrin.

Afterwards, as they consumed a Thai takeaway, Eleri was resigned to learn that Toby was among the people Vicky had invited round for a little get-together the following night. He had managed to get a job in another bank after much string-pulling on the part of friends and relatives, and had coaxed Vicky to ask him round whenever Eleri came up to town.

It was infinitely relaxing to talk into the small hours with someone she'd known since she was two years old. Later, in Vicky's spare bed, Eleri smiled to herself at the thought of the programme mapped out for next day, which, just as she'd told James, included a double bill at the cinema and an intensive tour of the shops—all of it under the same roof in Whiteleys.

They arrived back in Ealing at five, and took turns in the bathroom. Afterwards, Vicky, in a white jersey dress which clung to every curve, and Eleri, in a tangerine silk shirt and black velvet trousers splurged on that afternoon, were ready to confront the guests, and the kitchen was crammed with designer party food delivered while Eleri was in the bath.

Eleri suddenly felt extraordinarily festive as the first guests began to arrive, some of whom she'd met before, others who were new to her—particularly one large, red-headed man in black who insisted they remain together because they were so colour-co-ordinated as a pair. It was relaxing to indulge in a little harmless flirtation, knowing she looked good. Eleri thrust James from her mind, and set out to enjoy the evening to the full, her pleasure not in the least dimmed when Toby arrived, late and apologetic. Immaculate as always, his fair hair flopping over his forehead as he pushed his way through the throng, he detached Eleri skillfully from a brace of male companions.

'You won't mind if I steal her away?' he said, with a cherubic smile. 'Old friends, lot to catch up on.' He herded Eleri into a corner like a sheepdog, and stood over her as she perched on the arm of a chair. 'How are you?' he asked anxiously.

'I'm good.'

'I know you are,' he said ruefully. 'Good as gold, always.'

'How boring,' she said lightly.

'Seriously, Eleri, did that chap Kincaid take you back without any trouble?' Toby downed half his wine in one swallow, obviously nervous in the face of Eleri's serenity.

'Yes, he did. Eventually.' She sipped her own wine rather more sparingly. 'I walked out on him at first. As you well know, I was outraged by his suspicions. About the insider trading,' she added.

Toby coloured to the roots of his hair, and drank down the rest of his wine. 'But I know you're back at Northwold now.'

'Do you?' she asked curiously. 'Did Vicky tell you?'

'Er—no. I had it from someone else.'

'Who?' said Eleri, frowning.

Toby heaved a great sigh. 'My godfather told me.'

She stared at him, mystified. 'How on earth does he know about me?'

Toby shrugged. 'Old Godfrey sits on quite a few boards, including Northwold's. I asked him to breathe a word in Kincaid's ear. About you, I mean, to get you back poste haste. Got a lot of clout, my godpapa.'

Eleri thought through the list of names on the Northwold board of directors. 'By ''Old Godfrey'', I assume you mean Sir Godfrey Broadhurst, the property millionaire?'

Toby nodded. 'Told me never to pull a trick like that again. Chewed my ears off, in fact. But I didn't care a damn as long as I was able to put things right for you.'

'How very sweet of you, Toby.' Eleri looked up with a smile as the red-headed giant came bearing down on them, a glass in each hand. 'Is one of those for me?'

For the rest of the evening Eleri glittered like a Christmas tree, so vivacious that when the party was over Vicky asked in trepidation how many glasses of wine she'd downed.

'One and a bit. My effervescence was due to loss of temper,' Eleri assured her, eyes flashing. 'I, poor innocent that I am, have been labouring under the impression that James Kincaid asked me back to Northwold because he couldn't do without me. And all the while Toby—behaving altruistically for once—asked his godfather to bring pressure to bear on my darling boss. And because Sir Godfrey Broadhurst is a rich, very influential man, James did as he was told.' She turned a rather wild, glittering smile on Vicky. 'I suppose I should be grateful to Toby.'

'It wasn't Toby's idea,' said Vicky indignantly, pushing her hair up from her neck. 'It was mine. I bullied him into doing something after making such a pig's breakfast of your career and threatened to put the word out to all his friends if he didn't. Tell them what an unprincipled, thoughtless little—'

'So you were the one behind this?' Eleri let out a deep breath. 'I might have known. Not Toby's style at all.'

'I didn't mean to tell you,' said Vicky, grimacing. 'But I'm just not noble enough to let Toby take the credit.'

Eleri hugged her friend warmly. 'And why should you?'

'You're not angry with me?'

'Of course not—come on, let's clear this lot up.'

'No way. It can wait until morning,' said Vicky, and gave her a push. 'Get off to bed. Take some time off next trip and stay longer.'

'Thanks, I will.' Eleri grinned. 'Unless you acquire a flatmate in the meantime—male variety.'

'If I do it won't make any difference,' said Vicky, stretching luxuriously. 'He won't be occupying the spare bed!'

CHAPTER NINE

ELERI was so mad with James she gave serious thought to taking off on an early train next day. But that would have meant hassle for Vicky. Besides, she thought bitterly, she couldn't wait to confront him with her information about Sir Godfrey Broadhurst. She glowered as she remembered James's campaign to get her back to Northwold, all his talk of missing her and being unable to do without her. While all the time he'd been pressurised into reinstating her by a director of the board.

So promptly at four in the afternoon, when she spotted the Discovery slotting neatly into a parking space on the opposite side of the road, Eleri kissed Vicky goodbye and went down to intercept James Kincaid. It was very cold as she emerged from the building, with flakes of snow in the wind. Eleri greeted James politely, gave him her hold-all to stow away, then gave a wave up at Vicky's window and got in the car.

'Had a good time?' asked James. He was dressed in thick white sweater and faded moleskins, his feet in scuffed old chukka boots, and, to Eleri's annoyance looked just as good to her as always, perfidy or not.

'As usual with Vicky I had a fabulous time,' said Eleri truthfully.

'Including a double feature at the cinema?'

'Absolutely. Plus a shopping spree and a party at Vicky's in the evening. Toby was there,' she added casually.

'Was he indeed? Suitably apologetic for past sins, I trust?' he said acidly.

'Positively grovelling,' agreed Eleri, and changed her mind about hurling accusations at him for the moment. In bad weather the car was no place for a quarrel. 'I haven't heard a forecast. Is there likely to be much snow?'

'Worse in the north and west, I think. I'll keep the radio on to catch any traffic news. Don't worry. I'll get you home. The Discovery copes with most road conditions.'

'I'm not worried,' she assured him with truth. Angry, disillusioned—but not worried about her own personal safety. 'How was your weekend?' she added politely.

'I spent it in the Cartwright household, with children crawling all over me, including a couple of hours of apprehensive babysitting last night when Sam dragged my sister Helena out for dinner.' He sent a sidelong smile in her direction. 'Rather different from your evening, I imagine.'

'Very. Not that I mind babysitting. I've done it a lot in the past, when Nico was small. And my services will be in demand again shortly, when Claudia's baby arrives.'

'You're probably a damn sight more expert than me,' said James with feeling. 'My nephew woke up and insisted on coming down to watch television. I was too cowardly to refuse in case he made a fuss and woke his little sisters. A good thing Sam softened Helena up with champagne over their anniversary dinner—otherwise she'd have torn me to pieces when she came home to find the heir apparent watching football.'

Eleri chuckled involuntarily, finding it hard to picture James as a doting uncle. Or as a little brother. 'Is your sister much older than you, then?'

'Ten years. Not as much as you and Nico, but quite a gap when I was ten and she was at university. We get on better now we're older. She's mellowed a lot. My parents were astonished when Sam came on the scene and coaxed Helena into marriage. She was in her late thirties and totally wrapped up in her career.'

'What did she do?' asked Eleri with interest.

'University lecturer. Taught English Literature.' James slowed the Discovery a little, frowning as he peered through the windscreen at the thickening snow. 'I won't be able to make good time in this, I'm afraid. When are your family expecting you back?'

'I rang to say you were giving me a lift home, but I just said late evening. I usually add on an hour or two to save them worrying—' She broke off to listen to a weather flash.

Due to high winds and driving snow there had apparently been several accidents on the M4. Only one lane was open on the approach to the Bath turnoff, and already there was a twelve-mile tailback of westbound traffic in the area. Drivers were advised to find an alternative route.

James cursed under his breath. 'In this weather I'd intended to get as near Pennington as I could by motorway. But now I'll have to turn off at Swindon and chance our luck across country.'

Wishing more than ever that she'd returned by train, Eleri kept quiet. It seemed best to provide no distraction of any kind for James, who needed all his powers of concentration in the bad weather conditions. Fortunately the route was well known to him, and the four-wheel drive vehicle coped well, despite the gusting wind and thickening snow, but it seemed like hours to Eleri before they reached Cirencester.

'Not too far now,' said James, purposely cheerful, then shot a glance at her. 'Are you cold?'

'Just a bit.'

They said nothing more, all James's energies needed to steer them through the worsening blizzard. Another traffic flash informed them that some roads north of Stroud were blocked, and roads into Gloucester and Pennington were passable only with extreme care.

'Tell me about it!' growled James wearily as they crawled along at a snail's pace in a line of traffic. 'Eleri, a bit further on there's a turnoff to Compton

Priors. I vote we take it and make for the cottage. If we get stuck at least we can manage a couple of miles to Compton Priors on foot. If I try to push on to Pennington in this lot we might get stuck just the same, and be forced to spend the night in the car.'

Eleri shivered. 'Then by all means make for Compton Priors.'

He sighed impatiently as he indicated left and turned off on a side road. 'I'm sorry about this.'

'It's not your fault,' she said, trying to be fair. 'I can't help wishing I'd gone home by train, though.'

'Which is my fault. I can only apologise—' He broke off as the car slewed a little and he was obliged to use all his driving skills to prevent the car ending up in the hedge. 'Use my phone if you want, explain the situation to your parents.'

'I think I'll do that once we get to the cottage, so I can reassure my mother I've got a roof over my head.'

It took more than half an hour to negotiate the final couple of miles, and James was weary but triumphant when he parked the car in the lane outside Fosse Cottage at last. The village of Compton Priors was only a mile or so down the road, but in the whirling white darkness the cottage could have been in the wilderness for all the visible signs of habitation.

'Stay in the car for a minute, Eleri. I'll take our things in and open the place up.' James reached in the back for a large box, hefted both their bags, then jumped down into the white, howling night and disappeared up the path to his front door. Within seconds lights shone from the windows, and James came hurrying back to scoop Eleri out of her seat and carry her up the path.

'No point in getting wet feet,' he panted. He set her down in the small hallway, then slammed the door on the weather.

'Thank you.' Eleri closed her eyes in bliss. 'James—it's warm in here!'

He nodded. 'I've been leaving the heating to come on a couple of times a day in this weather, to avoid burst pipes. So far the electricity's holding up, thank the Lord. Let me have your coat.'

Eleri surrendered her jacket, which James hung amongst others on one of the iron coat-hooks behind the door. He raised a wrought-iron latch on one of the pair of doors flanking the front entrance and ushered her into a low-ceilinged room furnished invitingly with studded leather armchairs with velvet seats and a sofa covered in dark red woven material. A basket piled with logs stood on the hearth of a stone fireplace and lamps gleamed on tables on either side of the sofa. James crossed the room to draw dark red curtains across the windows, looking over his shoulder at Eleri.

'Do you like it?' he asked as she stood just within the door, still shivering a little, but more from reaction to the hair-raising journey than cold.

'It's lovely—very welcoming.' She gave him a wry little smile. 'Though tonight, in this weather, practi-

cally anywhere under cover would be welcoming too.
I don't mind confessing I was a bit nervous after we
left the motorway.'

'I wasn't too happy myself! I'll put the kettle on.
You need a hot drink.'

'I need a bathroom too, please, but before that I'd
like to ring my parents.'

James handed her his phone, then went out of the
room via a door at the far end, leaving her to explain
the situation to her mother.

'As long as you're safe I don't mind where you
are,' said Catrin, supremely practical as always. 'Better to spend the night in Mr Kincaid's spare bed than
in his car in a snowdrift.'

Eleri smiled at the pointed mention of a spare bed,
told her mother she'd keep her posted, then called
James back in.

He led her up a ladder-steep flight of uncarpeted
stairs which rose directly from the hall to a landing
with creaking, polished boards and three doors, one
of which opened on an austere bathroom with a claw-
footed tub and plain white porcelain fittings.

Left alone, Eleri lingered in the stark, but strangely
pleasing room, taking time to brush her hair and touch
lipstick to a mouth which still looked blue with cold.
Thankful she'd travelled in her warmest clothes, she
went back downstairs in search of James, and to the
right of the staircase found herself in a very masculine
study, with a large desk and a small iron grate flanked
by shelves stacked with books. Eleri went through the

far door into a large kitchen which stretched the entire width of the cottage at the back, with a conservatory opening from it.

'Come in,' said James. 'I thought you'd like some tea. Please sit down.'

He held out one of the wicker-backed chairs ranged round a plain pine table, and Eleri sat down to preside over the teatray he pushed towards her. To her surprise, James looked uncharacteristically ill at ease.

'What's the matter?' she asked bluntly. 'You seem on edge.'

'I think it's at this point I'd better confess that it was always my intention to persuade you to come here this evening on the way back to Pennington. Not,' he added hastily, 'under the same circumstances, it's true. I hadn't bargained for snow. Nor for spending the night. But I did bring along some provisions in the hope that we could share a meal and talk.'

Eleri, too surprised to answer for a moment, poured tea into tall beakers, enlightened now as to the source of fresh milk. 'What did you want to talk about?' she said guardedly. 'We see each other at Northwold. Couldn't we have talked there?'

James sat down opposite her and drank some tea. 'This has nothing to do with Northwold. It's purely personal. Besides, you haven't been very approachable lately. When I was ill I thought we'd drawn close, but once you started back at work you were a damn sight more distant than before.'

Eleri smiled placatingly. 'I was trying to be businesslike.'

'And succeeding. It was hard to imagine I'd ever held you in my arms—no—' he flung up a hand at her instinctive protest '—let me get this out in the open. The night I began to make love to you I lost my head and rushed things, but I didn't try to force you, Eleri.'

'I know,' she admitted, flushing. 'And probably if you—we—didn't work for the same company I might have gone to bed with you.'

'What utter rubbish,' he said flatly. 'I saw the look on your face, remember. For a few brief moments you were gloriously responsive—then suddenly you looked frightened out of your wits.' He leaned forward. 'I want to know why.'

For a moment the urge to explain, to confide in him was overwhelming. But what if he didn't understand, or, worse still, turned away from her in distaste? Eleri let out the breath she'd been holding and shook her head. 'You were mistaken—'

'No way!' he retorted vehemently. 'For a while you were as much on fire as I was. Then *wham*—the brakes were on full-stop, and from that moment on it's been perfectly obvious that all I can hope to get from you is efficiency and sweet, smiling civility. It makes working together bloody difficult. I persuaded you to come back so I feel responsible. Eleri, tell me the truth, do you really want to go on working at Northwold?'

She refilled her beaker with a steady hand, fighting to hide her dismay. 'In other words I must be more friendly to the boss or clear my desk again. Is that what you're saying?'

'*No!*' howled James, glaring at her. 'You know damn well it isn't. Don't put words in my mouth. I want you to stay—in fact I want you, period—no, hell I don't mean that.' He raked a hand through his hair. 'What I'm trying to say is that I love you. But being new to the emotion, I didn't realise it until you walked out on me. It wasn't your office skills I missed so badly, it was *you*.'

Eleri stared at him incredulously, then put her beaker down with a hand shaking so much in time to her pounding heartbeat she spilled some of the hot liquid on the table. She dabbed at it with a tissue. 'But what about Camilla—not to mention Venetia?'

James sat very still, his eyes narrowed. And to her annoyance he smiled crookedly, looked suddenly relaxed. While she was shaking from head to foot inside, she thought bitterly. Which was idiotic. She was in love with him, so the equation should have been simple. Only it wasn't, not in the slightest. If only he'd never come down with flu, or if Nico had taken his message, or she'd been less stupid at being unable to leave him alone and ill to fend for himself, they wouldn't be having this discussion.

'Camilla is a friend,' he said conversationally, 'a friend from way back. She wasn't in the least surprised when I told her there was someone else.'

'Venetia, I assume,' said Eleri acidly.

'No. You.' James sat back, arms folded. 'Venetia is a cousin. A married cousin who was in Pennington visiting her in-laws while her army husband is away playing war games in some uncivilised spot where she can't accompany him. He asked me to rescue her for one of the evenings she was here with his family. So I did. I didn't intend taking her to the trattoria, but we were walking past after a trip to the theatre and I caught a glimpse of you and acted on impulse.' He leaned forward suddenly, his eyes boring into hers. 'I was puerile enough to want to make you jealous. Did I?'

'Oh, yes,' said Eleri bitterly. 'You certainly did. Especially as I thought Camilla was still in the picture.'

'She is. I'm fond of her.' He smiled. 'It is possible to have friends of the opposite sex, Eleri. I want you for a friend too, but in your case I want a lot more than mere friendship. And,' he added, 'I intend to achieve it.'

Eleri sat back in her seat, looking at him steadily as her pulse slowed. 'So you begged me to come back to Northwold because you missed me not only for my value as an assistant but for the pleasure of my company?'

'Yes. When I was ill and you insisted on staying to look after me I realised that this was the element missing from my life. A woman of depth and compassion to share it. In short, you, Eleri.'

'So you didn't coax me back because Sir Godfrey Broadhurst told you to?' she said swiftly.

James stared at her, thunderstruck. 'No, I damn well didn't! How the blazes do you know about that, anyway?'

'He's Toby Maynard's godfather.' Eleri explained how Vicky had bullied Toby into using one of his innumerable contacts to get Eleri reinstated at Northwold.

'I wondered why the atmosphere was so arctic when you got in the car today,' said James bitterly. 'Maynard at work again.'

'Are you denying that Sir Godfrey asked you to reinstate me?'

'No, I'm not.' James got up, suddenly so aloof and remote she felt a sharp pang of dismay. 'But think back a little, Eleri. I was against your resignation in the first place. I knew there had to be an explanation about the blasted takeover information. I asked you to stay, or have you forgotten that?' His eyes glittered coldly. 'Amazing. I've never told a woman I loved her before. Conceited fool that I am, it never occurred to me that the object of my passion would receive the statement with total apathy—'

'Not apathy,' she muttered, flushing.

'What, then?' he demanded.

'I don't *know*!' she said in desperation, her heart hammering so hard she could hardly speak. 'Amazement, disbelief—'

'Disbelief? I thought I'd made it laughably plain

how I felt. I came chasing after you at the coffee-shop, lured you out to dinner on the pretext of talking business. I even arranged a party designed to tempt you back to Northwold.' He gave a mirthless laugh. 'In the event my dose of flu brought us nearer together than any party would have done. But although I got you back, much good it's done me. I thought if I had you with me every day I could make you see how important you were to me. In every aspect of male/female relationship. Partners of the heart as well as professionally. Bloody fool, wasn't I? Never more so than when my base male feelings got the better of me one night. You were like some Victorian maiden affronted by my lust.'

'I'm neither Victorian, nor a maiden,' said Eleri with sudden violence. 'Nor did I have the least idea that—that—'

'I'm in love with you,' he put in conversationally, watching with interest as colour flooded her face.

She thrust her hair behind her ears with trembling hands. 'I still find it hard to believe.' She smiled at him shyly and James took in a deep, unsteady breath.

'Would it be too much to ask about your feelings for me?'

'No.' So dizzy with joy that he loved her, Eleri was ready to tell him anything he asked. 'At the risk of making you conceited, I put you up on a pedestal, James Kincaid. But you wobbled a bit when I heard about Sir Godfrey. I'm only human.'

James came round the table and pulled her to her

feet. 'Eleri. Do you remember putting Sir Godfrey through to me on the phone last Monday?'

'Yes.'

'That was when he asked me to reinstate the lady young Toby Maynard had told him about. It was a bit late in the day, he admitted, but it had slipped his mind.' James's grasp tightened cruelly on her wrists. 'It gave me great pleasure to tell him that there'd never been any question of your losing your job.'

Eyes incandescent, Eleri reached up and kissed his cheek, rather startled when James stiffened at her touch. He dropped her hands and turned away briskly, the air of importuning lover falling from him like a cloak.

'Right. Time we had something to eat. You must be hungry.'

Feeling as though she'd been dropped suddenly from a great height, Eleri stood still, bemused, incredulous elation fizzing through her veins like champagne.

'Tell me what you brought and I'll do a meal,' she said, pulling herself together.

James gave her a look which brought the colour to her face, then began to unpack the box of food. 'I hope you're lost in admiration of my will-power. We'll return to the subject of our mutual feelings after supper.'

Helena Cartwright had packed bread, cheese, eggs and thick rashers of bacon, tomatoes, mushrooms, fresh pasta, and an apricot tart.

'Made,' said James, 'by her own hand. For an academic she's a fair cook. I hope it wasn't intended for Sam's dinner tonight.' He gave her a friendly smile totally at odds with the heat in his eyes. 'How about a good old fry-up? I'm starving.'

By the time Eleri had inspected the store-cupboard and the oven she had her emotions well in hand—other than a certain irrepressible excitement. With a speed fuelled by hunger she set about heating the grill and a frying pan to achieve a meal as quickly as possible, instructing James to lay the table and slice bread. Within a miraculously short time they were both tucking into two sizzling platefuls of food, taking care to ignore the emotional tension still heavy in the air between them.

James talked about his parents' home in Provence during the meal, and Eleri, not sure whether he'd regretted his outburst or was simply giving her breathing space, listened quietly as he described the lavender-filled garden and white-shuttered house his parents had bought years before, ready for retirement.

He put down his knife and fork at last with a sigh of pleasure. 'That was wonderful. I was allowed a lie-in this morning after my babysitting labours, so I ate a sort of brunch at mid-morning and nothing since. How about you?'

'Just toast and coffee about the same time,' she admitted. 'Could I make some more tea?'

'Just sit there. I'll do it.' While the kettle boiled

James opened the back door to take a look outside, and came back in hurriedly, shivering. 'Still snowing like blazes out there. The wind's risen even higher, too.' He made tea and brought the tray over to the table. 'How about some of Nell's apricot tart?'

Eleri shook her head regretfully. 'I shouldn't have pigged out on the bacon and eggs. I don't have room. I'll just wash these plates—'

'Don't bother. Stick them in the dishwasher. But first I'll take the tray into the sitting room and put a match to the fire.'

Eleri cleared the table and put everything away, aware in every fibre of the intimacy of their situation. They were isolated from the world for the time being. When the kitchen was tidy Eleri went into the sitting room and closed the door behind her. James was hunkered down on his heels in front of the fire, adding more logs. He turned to look up at her with a smile.

'Come and sit down, Eleri. I don't have a television here, I'm afraid.'

'Good. Makes a nice change.' She poured tea, trying not to think of later when it would be time for bed. She leaned over to hand him his cup, then sat back, sipping from her own, her eyes on the dancing flames. 'It's very peaceful here.'

'That's the snow. Normally we get quite a bit of traffic through here in the evenings, due to the excellent food served in the village pub.' James got up and sat down in one of the leather chairs. 'Though good food isn't quite the draw for you that it is for some, I imagine.'

'No.' Eleri smiled. 'Frankly I enjoyed our fry-up more than anything I've eaten in a long time.'

'Not a girl to be put off by dramatic scenes, then,' he observed dryly.

'It's a long time since I was a girl,' she said obliquely.

'You're not even thirty yet!'

'True. But some women are ''girls'' well into middle age. I'm not one of them.'

James shook his head. 'No, you're not. You're an intelligent woman with the type of good looks which last into old age.'

'Thank you. Though I wasn't complaining—merely stating the obvious.'

There was silence in the room while they both stared into the flames. Then James reached forward to put on more logs, and when he sat down again he took the space on the sofa beside her instead of returning to his chair. He took one of her hands in his and held it tightly.

'So what are we going to do, Eleri?'

'Do?' she said, startled.

'I wasn't suggesting a game of charades or a hand of bridge,' he said with sarcasm. 'I was referring to what happens tomorrow when we get back to Northwold.'

Eleri wondered if his fingers were registering her

galloping pulse. 'We may not get back there tomorrow.'

'If not tomorrow, the next day. One way or another life will go on,' he said inexorably. 'I'm merely asking how you want affairs to proceed.'

'I'm not sure what you mean—'

'Don't be coy, Eleri. It's not your style.' James turned to look at her. 'It can't have escaped your memory that only a short time ago I made a declaration of love. It may have been untimely, and in many ways I wish I'd kept my mouth shut, but the fact remains that for the second time in our association I've uttered three little words which shocked the living daylights out of you. I might just as well have saved my breath on both occasions for all the good it did me.'

Eleri stared back at him, unable to tear her eyes from the bright, searching gaze she knew so well. 'You mean that having said that—that—'

'I love you,' he prompted.

'Do you mean,' she went on with care, 'that you won't want me to stay on at Northwold?'

James glared at her, incensed, and tossed her hand back into her lap. 'Is that all you can think about? Your *job*?' He swore colourfully, and jumped to his feet. 'I need a drink. Can I get you one?'

'Yes, please.'

'What would you like?'

'I don't know—anything.'

James seized the tray and went into the kitchen,

leaving Eleri in despair, wondering how to tell him that his sentiments were returned in full. Her chin lifted as he came back into the room with a glass in each hand.

'The choice was limited,' he said shortly. 'I've got Scotch, but I know you dislike that so I brought you some dry sherry.'

'Thank you.' She took it from him, feeling it was hardly the time to tell him that she loathed dry sherry even more than whisky.

James resumed his seat beside her and sat staring morosely into the fire. 'You obviously feel you can't continue working with me now.'

Eleri downed some of her drink like a dose of medicine. 'I didn't say that.'

He threw a brooding look at her. 'So what are you saying?'

'I want to go on working for you. Unless,' she added, sitting straighter, '*you* don't want that.'

'What I want and what I'm going to get are obviously two different things,' he growled, and slumped lower in his corner of the sofa. 'Hilarious, really. I've known quite a few women at one time or another—most of them more beautiful, and all of them more willing. Why in heaven's name must you be the one I can't do without!'

Eleri stared at him, then began to laugh helplessly.

'I can't help it,' she gasped. 'It was such an outrageously back-handed compliment. It almost convinces me you mean it.'

'Of course I damn well mean it, Eleri,' he said with controlled violence. 'It's not the type of thing one says lightly. For me, anyway. What the devil can I do to convince you?'

She ran the tip of her tongue round dry lips, her laughter suddenly gone. There was a very easy way to convince her if James would only stop talking and make love to her. She was about to tell him so in words of one syllable, when the lights went out.

CHAPTER TEN

THE flames from the fire gave them enough light to see by as James, cursing volubly, made for the hall to check the trip switch. He came back in the room, shaking his head at Eleri's look of enquiry.

'No such luck. It does trip sometimes, in a thunderstorm, but I suppose it was too much to hope for on a night like this. Probably the whole neighbourhood's out. I'll ring the pub.'

A brief conversation with the landlord confirmed that the Boar's Head was functioning on an emergency generator and the rest of the village was in darkness.

'How are you off for logs?' said Eleri as James came back from the kitchen with a pair of candles stuck on saucers.

'Stacks of them. I also,' he added smugly, 'possess a small camping stove, so you can even have some more tea if you want.'

'What more can I ask?' she said, smiling.

'What indeed?' he said dryly, and looked at his watch. 'Almost eleven. It might be a good idea to get to bed soon, while we're still warm. Separately, of course,' he added suavely. 'The beds are made up, but they'll be cold. I don't possess a hot water bottle.'

'Can you spare a pair of socks?'

'Of course—good idea.' He gave her a grin which turned into a sudden yawn. 'Sorry. Must be the fire.'

'You're probably tired after that nightmare drive,' she said, and got to her feet. 'I shan't bother about more tea, thanks. I'll take myself off to your spare room and let you get to bed.'

'Right.' James picked up the candles and handed her one. 'Follow me.'

He led her upstairs to the door next to the bathroom. 'I'll go in first and put this somewhere so you can see.'

The room was small, and in the dim light it was hard to make out anything other than the bed and a dressing table. James put the candle down in front of the mirror, and pointed out her hold-all on a chair. 'Pretty basic, I'm afraid, but I've put an extra quilt on the bed and there are more blankets in the wardrobe over there.'

'I'll be fine,' she assured him, trying to find some way of asking him to stay with her. But the words refused to come out, and after a moment's hesitation James put out a hand to touch her cheek. 'Goodnight, Eleri. Sleep well.'

'Goodnight.'

She listened to his footsteps on the stairs, then fished in her hold-all for her toilet things and went to the bathroom, candle in hand. Shivering, she made swift preparations for the night then hurried back to her room. She tore off her clothes, pulled on a sweatshirt and leggings, then blew out the candle and dived into bed.

A knock on the door brought Eleri upright again, her heart pounding.

'I've brought the socks,' said James outside the door.

'Come in—but be careful, it's dark.'

James came over to the bed, candle in one hand. He chuckled. 'All I can see are two enormous eyes and a mop of hair.'

'It's too cold even to put my nose out,' she said, shivering, and reached out a hand to take the socks. 'Thank you.'

'My pleasure. Goodnight again.'

'Goodnight.'

When he'd gone, Eleri reached down in the bed and pulled on the socks, then curled up in a ball with the covers over her ears. Downstairs, in the warmth from the fire, she'd felt sleepy. But a session in James's ice-cold bathroom had put paid to any drowsiness, and now she felt wide-awake. Gradually her eyes grew used to the darkness, and she lay staring at the grey light filtering through the window, cursing herself for a fool. James, it seemed, hadn't felt like risking rejection a second time. Other than shaking her when she laughed at him he'd hardly touched her, except to hold her hand. The next move, if there was one, obviously had to come from her.

Eleri tried in vain to sleep. She heard James come upstairs, and water running in the bathroom, but after that there was nothing. Any faint hope that he might join her was gone. She tossed and turned and grew gradually colder. And after what seemed like hours it became necessary to make another visit to the bathroom. She hadn't thought to ask James for matches to relight the candle and had to grope her way across the creaking floor in the dark. When she emerged from the bathroom she gave a shriek as she cannoned into a hard, warm body.

James grabbed her and held her close. 'Sorry. I heard you get up and wondered if anything was wrong.'

'Sorry to wake you,' she muttered into his chest.

'Did you honestly believe I'd sleep?'

'I couldn't either. I was so cold. I'll never get to sleep on my own.' She heaved in an unsteady breath, then said in a rush, 'Can I come in your bed?'

Before the words were out of her mouth James had picked her up and was carrying her to his room. She clung to him, her arms round his neck and her face buried against his throat.

'Are you laughing again?' he demanded fiercely. She nodded as he thrust her into his bed and got in beside her. She turned to him, burrowing against him, and his arms closed round her. 'So tell me the joke, Eleri,' he ordered hoarsely.

'I'm just glad it's dark,' she said unsteadily. 'I've never tried to seduce a man before—I'm not dressed for the part.'

James ran a hand over the fleecy material covering

her breasts, then moved on down to the leggings and his own cricket socks. He shook with laughter. 'I see what you mean—well, not *see* exactly—'

'Just as well—'

'It doesn't matter a damn what you're wearing.'

'Good, because it's not very alluring.'

'You've got all the allure I can handle just the way you are,' he said roughly, and turned her face up to his. 'I almost begged to stay when I brought you the socks.'

'I wish you had.'

'I wish I'd known you wanted me to.'

'I was going to tell you how much downstairs. But the lights went out.'

James swore under his breath. 'So we've wasted at least two hours trying to get to sleep, when all the time we could have been together?'

'So let's not waste any more—kiss me!' she said crossly, and James gave a crack of delighted laughter and did as she ordered.

The moment their lips touched the laughter was over, and Eleri wondered feverishly how she could have felt so cold only a short time before. His seeking mouth was hungry, and she gave him back kiss for his kiss, the longing building inside her so rapidly she revolved her hips against him in shameless entice-ment. He took in a great gulp of cold air and held her still, his fingers digging into her hip-bones, then he began to caress her, his hands learning the shape of her in the dark, demonstrating why her choice of nightwear was immaterial as he dispensed with it summarily along with his own.

The cold of the night was forgotten as Eleri responded to him with such uninhibited ardour she felt a rush of triumph when James was so obviously forced to fight for control, striving to slow things down as he used all the skill he possessed to prolong their lovemaking. Eleri gasped and writhed as he kissed and caressed every inch of her body, wanting him so much she gasped in protest as he tore himself away for a moment. Then he turned back to her, sliding her beneath him, and kissed her fiercely as their bodies merged together at last, seeking each other in question and answer until they blended in a rhythm which brought them all too soon to the culmination Eleri experienced before him. She uttered a hoarse little cry of wonder, then clutched his head to her breasts in fierce possession as James surrendered himself to his own release.

Held close in each other's arms, shaken by their united heartbeats as their breathing slowed, it was a long time before James raised the head he'd buried against her throat. He reached out a hand to touch her face.

'Warmer now?' he whispered, and she laughed huskily.

'Yes. You're much better than a hot water bottle.'

'What a romantic little soul you are!'

'Are you seeking praise?'

'Not praise, exactly.' He inched up the bed and

held her close, drawing the covers over them. 'I suppose I'm asking if it was as miraculous for you as it was for me.'

'A lot more, probably.'

'I seriously doubt that.'

'Why?'

'Because I love you, Eleri. It's as simple as that.'

She curled closer, muttering something unintelligible into his neck.

'What did you say?' he demanded, turning her face up to his.

'I said,' she repeated desperately, 'that I love you too. I've been in love with you from the first day you arrived at Northwold—where are you going?'

James had leaned out of bed and was searching on his bedside table. He struck a match and lit a candle, then brought the candlestick over until the light shone full into her flushed face.

'Say it again!'

She put up a hand to shield her eyes. 'Blow it out, James—*please*!'

'Not until you tell me all that again.'

She felt the blood rush to her face, then, stammering over it a little, she repeated what she'd said before. 'Now put the light out!'

James blew out the candle and returned it to the bedside table, then slid down in the bed and kissed her until her head reeled. 'If,' he growled menacingly, 'you've loved me all that time, why have you been so damn difficult?'

She stiffened. 'Difficult?'

'Yes! Tonight, downstairs, I told you I loved you. And, as I mentioned at the time, it's not something I've ever told a woman before. Couldn't you have put me out of my misery—told me that you felt the same for me? It was a hellish daunting experience to confess my love to someone who never even flickered an eyelash in response.'

'I was dumbfounded, I suppose. Then when I was about to admit I felt the same the power went off and—well, the moment sort of slipped away.'

'So if you hadn't happened to need a visit to the bathroom tonight we would still be cold and sleepless, alone in our separate beds.'

Eleri shivered and he held her closer, moving his lips over her face. 'I honestly never thought I'd feel like this about any woman,' he said huskily. 'Do you believe me now?'

She nodded wordlessly.

'Enough to let you back to your own bed if that's what you really want.'

'No!'

'If you stay here you know what will happen. In fact—'

'You want to make love again right now.'

'Correction. I want to make love to *you* again right now. There's a difference.'

Eleri let out a long, unsteady sigh and reached up to pull his head down to hers. She kissed him long and hard and exulted as she felt him grow taut against her. 'I love you, James,' she whispered. 'I love the difference too—'

Eleri woke late next morning to find herself alone in a strange room in a bed she could now see was wide and rather beautiful, with a headboard carved from dark wood. The rest of the room was furnished sparsely, with a chest and wardrobe in the same dark wood, rugs on the polished boards of the floor and heavy dark red curtains at the multi-paned windows. Since the dressing gown draped over a chair matched the curtains, James, she thought, smiling, was obviously partial to red. Eleri stretched blissfully in the bed, wondering where he was, and braced herself to get out to make a trip to the bathroom. She snatched up his dressing gown and wrapped herself in it, then looked for the socks discarded in such haste the night before. She pulled them on then went to one of the windows, to find a white, silent world outside with a grey sky ominous with the threat of more snow.

Eleri raced through a chilly top-to-toe wash, brushed her teeth and slapped moisturizer on her face, and was attacking her wildly dishevelled hair with a brush when James knocked on the door.

She flung it open and smiled at him so radiantly he blinked and caught her in his arms, kissing her with a relish she responded to with fervour.

He raised his head, and smiled at her possessively.

'I've never meant good morning half as much before.'

'I know what you mean,' she assured him happily. 'I borrowed your dressing gown.'

'It looks better on you. In fact...' James held her away and ran his eyes over her from head to foot. 'You look wonderful.'

'I feel wonderful.' She shivered a little and burrowed close against him. 'But a bit cold, though.'

'The power's still off, so throw your clothes on and come downstairs; I've lit the fire.'

Eleri dressed at top speed, and ran downstairs to find a blazing fire and a tray ready laid for breakfast on one of the tables.

James came in from the kitchen with a coffee-pot in his hand and set it down, then took her in his arms and kissed her again. 'I was steeling myself to cope with the uptight Miss Conti again this morning,' he said into her hair, 'full of regrets for her night of abandon.'

She tipped her head back, smiling up at him. 'Not a bit of it. I loved every minute of last night, waking and sleeping—once I was in *your* bed, at least. I was gradually freezing to death in the other one.'

'So you let me make love to you just to get warm!'

Eleri pushed him away, sniffing the coffee with anticipation. 'There wasn't much letting about it, James Kincaid.'

'True,' he agreed with relish. 'Let's pull the sofa nearer the fire. I've done some bread and butter, but no toast, I'm afraid. And I thought we ought to hang onto the eggs in case we need them later. By the look of the weather we're not going anywhere today.'

'A good thing you've got a camping stove,' she said with fervour as she sipped the coffee. 'How far is it to the village?'

'About a mile.'

'Is there a shop there?'

'Yes. One of a disappearing breed, a post office stores.' He smiled at her caressingly. 'By the way you're wolfing down the bread you're obviously hungry.'

She flushed a little. 'Yes.'

'Making love most of the night does make one hungry, my darling.' James's eyes softened as they took in her heightened colour.

'I've never—' She stopped, biting her lip.

'Never what?'

'Made love all night before. I didn't think it was possible.'

James threw back his head and roared with laughter. 'Anyone would think you were thirteen, not rising thirty—now what have I said?'

Eleri smiled brightly. 'Nothing. More coffee?'

They sat in silence for a while, then James took her cup and put it back on the tray with his own. He turned to her and pulled her onto his lap, and held her close.

'I still can't quite believe this is happening,' she sighed, gazing into the flames.

'But it is,' he said gloatingly, and turned her face

up to his. 'And whether we want to be or not we're marooned here until the weather improves. I went down to the car earlier on and it's half buried in a snowdrift.'

'So Northwold will have to manage without us,' she said with glee.

'And without a few other people too, at a guess. Only those who live close by are going to make it into the plant today. A good thing we got the new launch up and running last week.'

'I'd better ring my mother again, tell her I won't be back until—when?'

'Can't say. No radio, television, newspaper—and the phone's dead too. Without my trusty mobile we'd be totally cut off.' James bent his head and kissed her suddenly. 'A situation I find totally to my taste in present company.'

Eleri returned the kiss with enthusiasm, then drew back to smile at him. 'It might pall when the food runs out.'

James grinned, and got up to put more logs on the fire. Then he paused, and put them back in the basket. 'Feel like a walk into the village? Rough going, but we could lay in a few supplies. I could go on my own if you don't feel up to it—'

'I'd love to come.' Eleri jumped to her feet. 'That way we might get some idea of how long our idyll is likely to last.'

He took her hands in his. 'You think of it as an idyll, then, darling?'

'Oh, yes.' She reached up to kiss him. 'The real world will pull us back soon enough, so let's enjoy today.'

'And tonight,' he said huskily, and pulled her close for a minute, then thrust her resolutely away. 'Any more of that and a walk will lose its appeal.'

'The dishwasher's no use now, so we wash up before any walk!'

'No, we don't. We save the dishes until we have a bowlful. We have to heat the water, remember! Now give your mother a ring, and then let's get going.'

The selection of boots in a broom cupboard included an old pair of Helena's. With an extra pair of socks inside them, James's sailing waterproof over her jacket and her own fur-lined gloves, Eleri felt ready for whatever the weather could throw at her. James, in old hiking boots, with a wool scarf at the neck of a much-worn Barbour and a shapeless tweed hat pulled low over his eyes, locked the cottage behind them and they set out to make their way along the partially blocked road to Compton Priors.

When they reached the village at last the store was full of people on the same mission. The forecast wasn't all that promising, they were told, with little likelihood of restored power before next day, and even then only if the snow held off. James had been coming to Fosse Cottage since early childhood, and knew most of the customers. He introduced Eleri all round, explaining their situation, whereupon people asked if they were all right for firewood, told them the garage could provide an extra canister for the camping stove and offered advice about burst pipes.

Laden with carrier bags of supplies, Eleri and James slithered their way back to the cottage, by which time it was early afternoon and snow was coming down thick and fast again.

'I don't know about you, but I'm done in,' panted Eleri as she stamped snow off her boots in the little front porch.

James pulled her inside, dumped the bags down, then sat her down on the stairs so he could pull her boots off. 'I'll see to the fire first, then we'll have some lunch.'

Something easy and quick was voted on, with anything more ambitious to be kept for their evening meal. Eleri opened two large tins of asparagus soup and put them to heat on the little stove while she put the rest of the food away. She hummed happily as she sliced bread, and suddenly James came up behind her and slid his arms round her waist, rubbing his cheek against her hair.

'I'm very grateful to the snow,' he said in her ear.

'So am I.' She twisted round in his arms, her face rosy with exertion. 'This is all such fun.'

He grinned. 'No hot water for a bath, no light, no television or radio, a two-mile hike in the snow and the lady thinks it's fun!'

'Isn't it fun for you, too?'

'It's more than just fun.' He pinched her cheek

gently. 'I need that to convince myself this isn't a dream.'

'You're supposed to pinch yourself, not me!'

'More fun my way,' he assured her, then leapt across the kitchen to rescue the pot of soup. 'Like me, this is near boiling point.'

They ate their meal in front of the roaring fire, so comfortable in each other's company Eleri wished this out-of-time interlude could go on for ever.

After lunch she made a sauce from the tins of tomatoes bought that morning. Along with some good olive oil, garlic and tomato paste from the same source, she added a pinch of dried basil and began heating the sauce on the camp stove.

Then she brought the pan to the hearth in the sitting room, where James constructed an impromptu trivet of logs so that the sauce could simmer for a while without wasting any of their precious gas.

'Then tonight all I need to do is drop some of your sister's pasta into a pot of water, grate some cheese, and hey presto—supper,' she said jubilantly.

'Wonderwoman!'

They sat close on the sofa while the light faded, talking in the glow of the flames. Eleri felt sleepy after the gruelling walk followed by the hot soup. Secure and warm in James's arms, she found she couldn't keep her eyes open and fell into a deep, dreamless sleep. She woke, refreshed, to find herself stretched full-length on the sofa with a rug over her.

James sat reading by the light of the fire and a pair

of candles, and Eleri lay very still, gazing at the forceful profile limned against the firelight.

And as though she'd sent out a message to him James turned his head to look into her eyes. They gazed at each other without speaking. He put down the book, doused the candles, leaned forward and pulled the pan of sauce out of harm's way, then got up, holding out his hand. Without a word, Eleri reached up to take it, and he pulled her to her feet and led her from the room.

They mounted the stairs in total silence, and once in his bedroom she began taking off her clothes with dreamlike slowness, oblivious of the cold as she basked in the heat of the glittering gaze which followed every movement. When she was naked James seized her by the elbows and held her at arm's length, his eyes devouring every line of her, then suddenly he pulled back the covers and thrust her into the bed before stripping off his own clothes and sliding in to take her in his arms, both of them so aroused by the silent build-up to their lovemaking that this time there were no preliminary caresses, only a wild, frantic loving even more wonderful, in its own way, than before.

CHAPTER ELEVEN

WHEN Eleri was to look back on her interlude in the snow with James she would think of it as something as near perfection as any two mortals could hope for. They ate and slept, and in between made love more often than she'd have believed possible. They went downstairs for dinner that first night, but afterwards it seemed foolish to stay down and waste logs when they could keep each other warm in bed far more effectively. They lay entwined in the candlelight, discovering each other with questions and answers that taught each of them a great deal about the other, neither of them wishing to waste the hours in mere sleep. But because lying close together in bed had a tendency to make James want to stop talking and make love to her, they grew tired at last and fell asleep in each other's arms.

Eleri woke late next morning and knew at once that their idyll was over. The bedside lamp was on, and outside the world was cracking and dripping past their window. The thaw had begun.

'James,' she said, stroking his face. 'Wake up. The electricity's back.'

He groaned, holding her tightly. 'Switch it off. Let's stay here.'

She sighed. 'If only we could—'

Right on cue the phone began to ring. James reached out a bare arm and picked it up, barking his name.

He listened, then asked some brief questions.

'Right. I'll be in tomorrow morning.' He rang off and turned to Eleri morosely. 'Northwold, it seems, has not ground to a halt without us, but I gather our return would be much appreciated just the same.'

'Look on the bright side,' she said cheerfully. 'At least we can have a bath this morning. I'm tired of turning blue while I wash myself in bits why are you looking at me like that?'

'A bath,' said James, eyes glinting. 'Good idea. I'll join you.'

And, protest as much as she liked, Eleri couldn't dissuade him, with the result that the bathroom floor needed much mopping up afterwards and both she and James were blue with cold by the time they were dry and in their clothes, restored heating or not.

'That particular pastime,' said Eleri over breakfast, 'is just not possible until you get a bigger bath.'

James paused, a forkful of omelette halfway to his mouth. 'If I do will you come out here and share it with me?'

'Now and then, maybe.'

He resumed eating, suddenly businesslike. 'We won't be able to start back quite yet, so let's talk.'

Eleri poured coffee into their cups, frowning at him

across the table. 'I have a feeling I'm not going to like your subject.'

'I merely want to know where we go from here.'

She nodded glumly. 'I thought you might. Shall I tell you what I want?'

James looked taken aback. 'I thought it was more usual for the male half to take the lead in this kind of thing.'

'I don't see why!'

He threw up his hands. 'All right, don't flash those black Italian eyes at me!'

'Welsh, not Italian.' Eleri finished her coffee, eyeing him warily. 'Perhaps you'd better go first after all. My agenda might not find favour.'

'Mine's fairly simple.' He raked a hand through his hair, eyeing her with something less than his usual self-confidence.

'Go on,' she said quietly.

'I've never felt like this before,' he began with sudden urgency. 'I've known and liked a few women in the past, but I've never felt I couldn't live without any of them. You tell me you love me too—'

'And demonstrate it fairly comprehensively, I would have thought,' she pointed out.

'So much so,' he agreed, 'that it's taking a great effort of will on my part to remain this side of the table. But there's more to life than making love. I need commitment from you, Eleri.'

'Commitment,' she repeated expressionlessly.

'Yes.' He cleared his throat, then gave her an odd,

awkward smile. 'Whatever form of it you like best. A partnership, marriage—whatever you say.'

Eleri's heart leapt to her throat, then resumed its normal location, leaving her breathless. She thrust her hair behind her ears, looking at him beseechingly. 'Could you settle for a little less than that, for now?'

James let out a long, deflated breath. 'I tell you I love you and you stare at me, speechless. I propose and you ask me to settle for less. What kind of woman are you, Eleri? Do you take delight in chopping me down to size?'

'*No!*' She shook her head miserably. 'I love you, James. I love you desperately. I have since the moment I first met you. All I'm asking is that we don't rush into things.'

'I'm not suggesting we rush into anything. We can do the entire, conventional bit. Get engaged for as long as you want—' He stopped abruptly, eyes narrowed. 'Or is there some prior commitment of yours I don't know about?'

'Not exactly,' she said with difficulty.

James eyed her narrowly. 'Tell me what you mean, Eleri.' His eyes lit with comprehension suddenly. 'Are you married already? Is there a husband around who won't give you a divorce?'

'No.'

'Then what?'

'I can't tell you.'

'Why the hell not?'

'Because it involves—other people.' She got up

and went round the table to him, her eyes imploring, and James jumped to his feet, holding her off.

'No. Don't. If you touch me I'm lost.' He blinked rapidly. 'I can't believe you would do this to me.'

Eleri's hands fell to her sides. 'I'm sorry, James.'

'So what do we do now?' he demanded roughly. 'Carry on as though nothing has happened?'

'Couldn't we just go on as we are?'

'Which I'd be happy to do, if it means you were willing to live with me. But you're not, are you?'

'There's nothing I'd like more,' she said passionately. 'But my father—'

'You're a grown woman, Eleri, free to do as you want with your life.'

She gazed at him beseechingly. 'Theoretically, yes. But in my own case it just isn't possible.'

'Give me one good reason why.'

'I can't *do* that,' she said in anguish.

James looked suddenly haggard. 'Then there's no more to be said.' He flung away to open the door, and peered out at the dripping white day. 'It's likely to be a hairy ride, but to hell with it. I'd rather drive back than stay here in the circumstances.'

Eleri gazed in despair at his broad back. 'James. Please. Don't—'

'Don't what?' he said bitterly, slamming the door shut. He turned to look at her with cold, angry eyes. 'You slash me to ribbons then tell me not to make a fuss?'

'I would do anything not to hurt you,' she said

wildly. 'This is why I've never let myself get near anyone before. I thought I could avoid falling in love. And I did. Until I met you. Then I couldn't help myself.' To her horror tears welled in her eyes and spilled over.

With a choked sound James covered the space between them and took her in his arms. 'Don't cry,' he ordered huskily, rubbing her cheek against his. 'I've never seen you cry before. Stop, for God's sake—I can't handle it!'

Eleri gave a smothered sound somewhere between a sob and a chuckle, and pulled free, knuckling her tears away. 'Sorry.' She looked up at him. 'I'll go and pack, then.'

'Is that an oblique way of saying we've reached an impasse?' he demanded.

She breathed in deeply and squared her shoulders. 'James, I love you desperately. I probably will for the rest of my life. And I'll spend as much social time with you as you want, short of moving in with you, as well as working at Northwold. But if, as you say, you can't handle all that I'll hand in my resignation—officially this time—and take myself out of your life.'

'My God,' he breathed, staring down at her. 'You mean it too, don't you?'

Eleri nodded, sniffing inelegantly. 'I just wish we'd never made love. It's going to be so *hard*—'

'No, it isn't.' He caught her hands in his. 'All right, I had some crack-brained idea about driving you home and parting from you with a dignified goodbye.

But that doesn't happen in real life.' He smiled ruefully. 'Instead I think I'll come courting in the good
old-fashioned way. Maybe if your parents see my intentions are honourable they might fight my corner
for me.'

Whereupon Eleri hurled herself into his arms and
wept far more bitterly than before, and James crushed
her close and said a great many things she had never
in her wildest dreams imagined he'd say. At last he
put her from him gently and sent her upstairs to wash
her face and collect her belongings.

She was composed by the time she rang her mother
to say she was on her way home and warned her that
the journey might take some time because the roads
were still far from clear.

'All right, darling?' said James as he helped her
into the car.

'Yes.' She smiled at him, then looked back over
her shoulder at the cottage. 'Just sorry to leave here.'

'So am I.' He heaved a sigh as he got in the car.
'But civilisation demands our presence.'

They reached Pennington late in the afternoon, after a difficult journey through pouring rain, the resul-
tant spray from heavy goods vehicles making visibil-
ity dangerously poor on the faster stretches of road
back to the town. When they arrived at the house
James lifted Eleri down then reached for her bag and
waved her before him to her front door.

'At this time of day I assume your parents are probably home. I'd like to apologise to them personally for not getting you back to them on Sunday.'

Eleri quailed at the prospect, but one glance at James's implacable face decided her against any argument. Instead of using her key she rang the bell for once, and smiled involuntarily as Nico flung the door wide, a broad grin on his face.

'I saw the car—thought it must be you, El. Hi, James, you brought her back in one piece, then.'

'A bit late,' said James in wry apology. 'But safe and sound in the end. Are your parents in?'

'Sure. Come in.' Nico led the way down the hall towards the family sitting room. 'Ma, Eleri's home. James is with her.'

Catrin emerged from the kitchen, hurriedly removing a butcher's apron from her formal black dress. 'Thank goodness. I was beginning to get worried,' she said, hugging her daughter. 'Were the roads bad? Come in, come in, Mr Kincaid. Nico, go and call Papa. He's upstairs, changing.'

Within minutes James was installed on a sofa with Eleri, tea and scones pressed on them, while Nico fired questions about their journey in the snow.

'Good job it didn't start on Saturday,' he said with fervour.

'Might have cancelled your old football, I suppose,' said Catrin in disapproval. 'Have another of these, Mr Kincaid.'

'James, please,' he said, smiling at her, then got to his feet as Mario Conti came into the room, dressed formally for his evening at the trattoria. 'Good evening, Mr Conti.' He held out his hand. 'James Kincaid. I trust you'll forgive the intrusion. I'm here to apologise for marooning your daughter in the snow.'

Mario Conti took the large, capable hand, shook it formally, and waved James back to the sofa. 'I am only grateful you were able to get her to safety.'

To Eleri's surprise the encounter went off very well, with James very much at home with her family. Nico, of course, had already given James his personal seal of approval, but it was interesting to watch her parents responding to him with far more enthusiasm than accorded to any other of her men-friends in the past. But that was the point, of course, she reminded herself. They thought of him as her employer.

It was a full hour before James took his leave. He smiled at Eleri, told her he'd see her in the morning, then went out with Mario and Nico to see him to the door.

'I thought he'd be older than that,' said Catrin absently as she piled cups on a tray.

'Why?'

'I don't know. Maybe it's me, getting old. I didn't think a managing director would be so young.'

'He's late thirties, Ma. Not wet behind the ears, exactly.' Eleri took the plates into the kitchen, holding open the door for her mother.

'You never mentioned what an attractive man he is either.' Catrin cast a sharp glance at Eleri's tired, pale face. 'No hardship to be cut off by the snow with him, I fancy?'

'No,' agreed Eleri, unruffled. 'He's good company—and we've known each other quite a time now, remember.'

'How did you manage when the power was off?'

'Very well. We had a log fire to keep warm, and a camping stove to cook with.'

'How about food?'

'The village store provided that,' said Eleri, deciding not to mention the box of provisions James had brought with him. She yawned. 'You're both on duty tonight, I suppose. Shall I make Nico's supper?'

'No need. I did a chicken casserole and some rice. You just have to heat it up.' Catrin eyed her daughter searchingly. 'You look as though a good night's sleep wouldn't go amiss.'

Eleri nodded casually. 'My adventure in the snow was a bit tiring after my London spree.' She looked up as her father came in. 'James gone, Pa?'

'Yes.' Mario smiled a little. 'He is not at all what I expected, *cara*.'

'Did you like him, Mario?' asked his wife.

'Yes. I asked him to call again, whenever he wished.'

Next morning Eleri arrived at Northwold half an hour earlier than usual, and found James, as she'd hoped, alone at his desk in the deserted administration block. As she went in she closed the door behind her, and he jumped to his feet with a smile which turned her heart over.

'Shut the other door too,' he instructed softly.

Eleri obeyed, then walked into the arms outstretched to receive her and lifted her face to a kiss as hungry and protracted as though they hadn't seen each other for months.

'It's almost twenty-four hours since I last kissed you—I was suffering withdrawal symptoms,' he said huskily, when he raised his head. 'Good morning, my darling Miss Conti.'

'Good morning, Mr Kincaid,' she returned demurely.

He sighed and released her reluctantly. 'I'd better get back behind my desk before I ravish you on the carpet. Now I can exist reasonably well until tonight, when I kiss you again. I'm taking you out to dinner.'

Eleri sat down in her usual place, her eyes meeting his in appeal. 'I can't tonight, James.'

'But you know damn well I'm going to London in the morning to a meeting. I won't be back before late on Friday night!'

'Sorry.' She smiled placatingly. 'It's a big night tonight at home. Nico's bringing a girlfriend to supper.'

'A girlfriend! He's only fifteen,' said James in disapproval.

'Didn't you have a girlfriend when you were fifteen?'

'Lord, no. In my school we played a lot of energy-channelling games and took cold showers.' James frowned. 'Are there girls at Nico's school, then?'

Eleri nodded. 'The comprehensive in the town.'

'Is that where you went?'

'No. Claudia and I both went to St Ursula's, the convent school. High standard of education, but no contact with the opposite sex.' She smiled wryly. 'Nico's never shown much interest in girls up to now. We didn't know he had a girlfriend. So tonight my parents are having a night off from the trattoria, my father's going to cook the meal in honour of the occasion, and my presence is required.'

'By your parents?'

'No. Nico asked me. He thinks Lucy might not be so nervous if I'm there too.' She sighed, looking at him through her eyelashes. 'I'd rather be with you.'

'I'll take plenty of work home with me to keep me occupied,' he said grimly. 'And I'll leave plenty for you to do while I'm away too, madam. I don't want Bruce, or any of the others, monopolising your time.' He paused, rolling a pen between his fingers. 'What was your parents' verdict, by the way?'

'On you? They were impressed. According to my mother you're very young and attractive to be a managing director, and my father approved of your proper behaviour in coming to apologise for keeping me out in the snow.'

'Good,' he said smugly. 'I liked them both. With luck I'll soon have them on my side.'

'Don't you dare take any little short cuts with my family,' she warned, eyes flashing.

'I wouldn't dream of it,' he said silkily. 'I just thought I'd get them used to me by degrees. I think Nico approves already.'

'Oh, yes—he thinks you're cool.'

James leaned forward. 'He's wrong. The last thing I feel about you is cool. It was bad enough when I had no idea how you felt about me. But now, with the thought of you in my bed coming before me and my report to the board—'

'James!' Her face flaming, Eleri was prevented from giving the managing director a tongue-lashing by the arrival of Bruce Gordon, who came in to commiserate with James for being stuck in the snow.

James assured him it could have been a great deal worse. The cottage, he informed Bruce blandly, had been equipped with all the comforts a man could want—at which point Eleri excused herself hastily and left to get on with her day.

Eleri was glad of a period of quiet, both at Northwold and at home, while James was in London. It gave her time to think, to sort things out in her own mind before she saw him again. He asked her to stay on a little later each day in his absence, so he could ring her for a private talk out of earshot of either colleagues or family. The conversations grew so protracted that by Friday night Catrin was indignant about the amount of overtime her daughter was putting in.

'I thought you said James was away,' she said crossly, when Eleri arrived home. 'I had to wait for you before I could go over the road.'

'You needn't wait for me, Ma. I'm a big girl, you know.'

Her mother looked unconvinced. 'Talking of which, I've been thinking, *cariad*.'

'Always a dangerous pastime!'

'Be serious, girl. It's your birthday on Sunday.'

'I know.' Eleri pulled a face. 'A bit of a wrench, not being twenty-something any more.'

'Age is relative,' stated Catrin positively. 'Anyway, as your birthday falls on a Sunday, I thought we'd have a family meal, with Claudia and Paul as well, if the baby hasn't arrived. And I thought you might like to invite James.'

Eleri's eyes widened in dismay. *'James?'*

'Yes. Why not?'

Eleri thrust strands of hair behind her ears in agitation. 'I work for him. It wouldn't be the right thing to do.'

'I know very well you work with him, but you're in love with him too,' said her mother, rendering her daughter speechless. 'And, unless I'm very much mistaken, he feels very much the same about you.'

Eleri stared at her mother wildly. 'Why would you possibly think that?'

Catrin shook her head pityingly. 'Do you think I'm

blind, or too old to remember what it's like? When you were sat together on the sofa there was a sort of aura enclosing you both. Your father didn't notice it, of course, but Nico did.'

'All right, all right,' said Eleri in despair. 'But don't worry, I'm not going to do anything rash.'

'Perhaps it's time you did, Eleri Conti. It's certainly time you had a man of your own. And unless I'm completely wrong James is in complete agreement with me. He didn't touch you, of course. But, *duw*, he wanted to.'

'Oh, go away, you Welsh witch,' said Eleri, laughing.

'Life's too short to waste it, love,' said Catrin soberly as a parting shot, and went off to help her husband at the trattoria.

Nico came home from a visit to the cinema with his fair, pretty Lucy, and threw himself down in front of the television, eyeing Eleri's wet hair and towelling robe.

'No date tonight? I thought you might have been out on the razzle with James.'

'He's in London. You're home early.'

'Match tomorrow.'

'School?'

'Weren't you listening, El?' he said indignantly. 'I told you last night I'm playing for Pennington under-sixteens.'

'So you did. Sorry.' She rubbed at her hair, smiling apologetically. 'Want me to come along and cheer?'

'No need for the sacrifice. Lucy's doing the cheer-ing.' Nico looked at her. 'What's up, El? You look different since you came back from London. Is it James?'

'Yes,' she admitted warily. 'I like him very much.'

'*Like* him?' Nico hooted. 'You're nuts about him. And he's the same way about you. What are you go-ing to do about it?'

'I don't know—I haven't decided.'

He uncoiled himself and got up, yawning. 'Don't keep him hanging about too long. He might go off you.'

'Thanks a lot!' Eleri gave him a shove. 'Off to bed.'

Eleri lay full-length on the sofa when Nico had gone, stretching pleasurably at the thought of a whole Saturday with James. When the doorbell rang a few minutes later she looked up with a frown.

Putting down her book, she went out into the hall and along to the front door, opening the door only as far as the safety chain allowed. When she saw James standing there, grinning triumphantly, she slammed the door shut, removed the chain, then opened the door wide, her smile incandescent.

James closed the door behind him and took her in his arms without a word, kissing her until her head reeled.

'I couldn't wait until tomorrow,' he whispered. 'I took a chance on finding you alone.'

Eleri drew him into the sitting room, her eyes alight

with pleasure. 'I am. My parents are at the trattoria and Nico's gone to bed. I was just lazing here, thinking about tomorrow. Are you hungry?'

'No. I had something on the way home. All I want is this.' He picked her up and sat down with her on the sofa, kissing her all over her face. 'I like you all shiny-faced and warm from a bath. I could eat you. Have you missed me?'

'Yes. I told you that on the phone earlier.'

'This is better. Face to face, mouth to mouth...' There was silence for some time, until at last James put her away a little, smiling ruefully into her dazed, glittering eyes. 'No more or I'll disgrace myself and make love to you here and now on your mother's sofa.'

'I'd like that,' she murmured, and trailed a hand down his face.

He caught it, kissing the palm. 'What time are you coming round tomorrow? Or shall I come here and fetch you?'

'No. I'll drive over. When do you want me?'

'Right now.'

Eleri pushed him away, laughing. 'I'll come round about midday. Shall I cook lunch?'

'No. I'll make you a sandwich with my own fair hands. We'll go out for a meal in the evening.' He got up and pulled her to her feet. 'I'd better go. I don't want to alienate your parents after making such a good start the other day.'

Eleri went with him to the door, melting into his

arms with such uninhibited warmth to say goodnight it took James very obvious, gratifying effort to tear himself away.

'Go straight to bed and get some sleep,' he ordered. 'And don't be late!'

CHAPTER TWELVE

JAMES was waiting impatiently when Eleri arrived promptly at noon next day.

'You're late,' he accused, and stifled her indignant protests with a kiss so lengthy and possessive she was flushed and untidy by the time he set her free.

'I'm on time, not late. Hello, James,' she said pointedly, and he grinned.

'Hello, Eleri—' He broke off, eyeing the small hold-all which had dropped to the floor, unnoticed. 'Hallelujah! Does this mean what I hope it means?'

'No. You said you were taking me out to dinner, so I brought something rather more appealing to wear than this.' She waved a hand at her pink sweater and faded jeans.

'You look appealing to me in anything. Even more so,' he added, reaching for her again, 'in nothing at all. Come to bed.'

'Certainly not,' she said severely, dodging away. 'I was promised a sandwich, remember. I'm hungry.'

James sighed theatrically and led her into the kitchen, where a covered platter of sandwiches waited, with so many varieties of both bread and fillings that Eleri eyed him suspiciously.

'Dear me, you *have* been busy.'

He shook his head, grinning. 'I went shopping. But not only for sandwiches. Let's eat, then I can show you my other purchases later.'

To show her he'd been teasing about bed, James made it clear he was content to linger over lunch, happy just to be alone with her again. It was mid-afternoon before there was any discord in the harmony. They were together on the sofa in James's study when he fished in his pocket and drew out a small box.

'I suppose I should have asked your preferences first, but the moment I saw it I thought it was perfect. You can change it for something more modern if you like.'

Eleri stared at the ring, lusting for it so much after one look she wanted to snatch it from the box.

'You don't like it,' he said expressionlessly.

She looked at the band of rubies and diamonds through a haze of tears. 'No I don't *like* it,' she agreed huskily. 'I absolutely adore it. But I can't wear it, James. Everyone would know.'

'Exactly. It's the object of the exercise.' He took the ring from the box and slid it on her finger. 'It fits.'

'Perfectly.' Eleri looked at the ring in longing, then slid it off again and handed it to him. 'That wasn't fair, James.'

'Not fair?' He glared at her. 'What the hell do you mean?'

'You were jumping the gun. I told you I couldn't

give you the commitment you wanted. Not yet. We agreed—'

'No! *You* agreed. I still feel the same as before. Given the choice, I'd rush you to a register office tomorrow. Failing that, I'm doing the next best thing.' His eyes speared hers. 'Why won't you wear it?'

Eleri thrust her hair behind her ears despairingly. 'I never dreamed you'd want to go public yet. I meant it to be a secret just for you and me.'

James got up, his face so hard with suppressed anger she went cold. 'Why, for God's sake? How long do you intend keeping this up? Weeks? Months?' He paused at the stricken look on her face, then yanked her to her feet, his eyes stabbing hers.

'If I'm to be kept dangling indefinitely I need to know why. Tell me what this is all about.'

'I *can't*,' she said hoarsely. 'And if you can't accept that there's no point in going on.'

James stared at her in disbelief, then grabbed her by the hand and pulled her along with him as he strode from the room.

'What are you doing?' she demanded, quailing at the look on his face.

'The only thing left to me!' he said through his teeth, and without warning slung her over his shoulder for the journey down to his bedroom, where he tossed her unceremoniously on the bed, keeping her captive with both hands either side of her as he glared down into her scarlet, incensed face.

'On previous occasions I trust you noted my care

for you in certain preliminary aspects of our love-making. This time—oh, no you don't!' He moved fast as Eleri made a dive to escape.

She found herself flat on her back again, this time with a large male body on top of her, every inch of it taut with anger and the desire to subdue.

'This time,' said James, his face only a fraction from her own, 'we'll dispense with all that. To be blunt, Signorina Conti, I intend to get you pregnant.'

'It won't do any good,' she spat at him, her eyes glittering scornfully into his. 'Do you honestly think I'd leave precautions to the male of the species?'

James stared down at her in distaste, all urgency vanished. After a moment he rolled over and got to his feet. 'Illogical, I know,' he drawled, 'but my libido finds your forethought distinctly off-putting—hinting, as it does, of strings of predecessors in your embrace.'

Eleri got to her feet wearily. 'Not strings—'

'Of course not,' he agreed suavely. 'You're strictly a no-strings lady. Odd, really. At one time my ideal woman would have been someone both passionate *and* wary of committed relationships—' He broke off as the phone rang. With a punctilious word of apology he picked up the receiver and said his name, listened for a moment then passed the phone to Eleri.

'It's Nico, *cariad*,' said her mother, sounding distraught. 'He's in hospital at the General—'

'*What?*' Eleri's eyes widened in shock. 'Why? Has he had an accident? What happened?'

'It was his match. He was trying to head the ball and connected with the goalpost instead. He's unconscious—'

'I'm on my way,' said Eleri tersely, and jumped to her feet, almost throwing the phone at James.

'What's happened?' he demanded.

'Nico's in hospital,' she said, brushing him out of the way, but James held onto her arm.

'I'll drive you there,' he said firmly. 'You're shaking from head to foot. You can't drive anywhere like that.'

Eleri stared at him blindly, then nodded. 'All right, but hurry up.'

Within minutes they were at the crowded casualty department of Pennington General Hospital. Directed to a cubicle, they slid between the curtains to see Catrin sitting beside the still figure in the bed. She jumped to her feet to embrace her daughter, smiling valiantly at James.

'Don't look like that, *cariad*,' she told Eleri. 'They expect him to come round any minute.'

Eleri took her mother's place by the bedside, grasping Nico's lax hand in hers. 'He's very pale,' she said in anguish, then turned to look up at her mother. 'Where's Papa?'

'He doesn't even know yet! He went to the suppliers for more glasses. I took a taxi here and left him a note.'

'Is there anything I can do, Mrs Conti?' asked James. 'Would you like some coffee? Eleri?'

Catrin refused, thanking him, but Eleri didn't even hear him. She sat motionless, her eyes on the bruised, pale face on the pillow.

'I'll just see if Mario's arrived,' said Catrin. 'Would you mind staying with Eleri, James?'

He smiled at her in reassurance. 'Of course not.' He remained standing behind Eleri after Catrin had gone, his hand on her shoulder tightening as Nico's eyelids flickered slightly.

'Hi, Nico,' said Eleri, sounding so composed James eyed her with approval. 'Wakey, wakey.'

The long black lashes lifted, and dazed blue eyes stared up into smiling black ones. 'Hi, Mamma,' he said faintly.

Eleri swallowed, but managed to keep her smile in place. 'It's me, Eleri. Mamma's slipped out for a minute.'

'Thought it was quiet!' He noticed James and smiled feebly. 'Hi.'

'You're supposed to head the ball, not the post,' said James, grinning, and Nico pulled a face.

'I don't know much about it—' His face cleared. 'But I remember scoring in the first half. Did we win?'

'How silly of me not to find out,' said Eleri acidly.

'So Sleeping Beauty's back with us,' said a nurse, coming through the curtains. 'A doctor's coming to check on you in a minute, Nico, but you look pretty good to me.'

'And you likewise,' said the patient, grinning at her.

'Nico!' remonstrated Eleri, lips twitching. 'There's obviously not too much wrong with *you*.'

At which point a desperately anxious Mario Conti arrived with his wife and Eleri, after a quick kiss for Nico, went outside with James. He found a seat for her at the back of the waiting room, eyeing her pallor with concern.

'There's a machine over there. Have some coffee.'

She nodded gratefully. 'Thanks. White, with one sugar.'

He smiled wryly. 'I know that by now, Eleri.'

When James got back with the drinks, they sat in silence for a while among the bustle and noise of the emergency department. Eleri's colour improved as she drank the hot liquid, and she smiled gratefully at James when he got up to dispose of their plastic beakers.

'How are you feeling now?' he asked when he returned.

'Better. Sorry to make such a fuss.'

'It wasn't a fuss, Eleri.' He looked at the clock. 'What happens now?'

'A doctor was about to examine Nico—' Eleri broke off as she saw her mother beckoning her.

'Go on,' said James. 'I'll stay here.'

When Eleri got back from a talk with her parents she eyed James rather uncertainly. 'Nico has to stay in overnight to make sure he's over the concussion, but he's complaining so much about it there's obviously not much wrong with him.'

'I assume Nico's not thrilled to be in hospital on a Saturday night,' said James with a grin.

'That's the problem. He's supposed to be taking Lucy to a party.' Eleri looked down at her shoes. 'My parents are going home now; both of them are determined to carry on at the trattoria as usual.'

'Then I suggest you come home with me,' said James with decision, and took her over to her parents. 'If you're sure there's nothing either of us can do,' he said to the Contis, 'I thought I'd take Eleri back to my place and give her some dinner.'

Mario Conti nodded. 'That is best. Do not trouble to cook. I will send a meal over for you.'

'Good idea, Mario. I know the address,' said Catrin, and kissed her daughter. 'Say goodnight to Nico, then off you go. I'll see you later. Goodnight, James.'

Eleri was silent on the short journey to Chester Gardens. James made no attempt to break the silence, but led her straight into the study and sat down with her on the sofa, drawing her close.

'Don't worry. Nico's a tough youngster. He'll be right as rain tomorrow.' He smiled down at her. 'He's also very lucky, Eleri, to have so many people caring for him. I can't see Helena getting so distraught about *her* little brother.'

Eleri closed her eyes for a second, then raised her

head to look at him defiantly. 'Nico's not my brother,' she blurted. 'He's my son.'

James's arm tightened convulsively about her, his eyes suddenly dark with shock. 'My darling girl—' He let out a long breath, then drew her onto his lap and smoothed her head against his shoulder as though she were a child. 'So that's it. I knew there was something, but I couldn't put my finger on it. Does he know, darling?'

Eleri shook her head, relaxing slightly at the endearment. 'No. But my parents think it's time he did. That's what they were telling me at the hospital. They said it was time Nico knew the truth.'

James put her away from him a little to see her face. 'Do you agree?'

'In principle, yes.' Her mouth twisted. 'But not in practice. It was hard enough to tell you. The thought of confessing to Nico scares me to death. I'm afraid he won't—won't feel the same towards me afterwards.' She shrugged forlornly. 'So now you know why I couldn't marry you yet, as much as I longed to. I'd promised myself I would wait until Nico was older before—'

'Before having a life of your own?'

Eleri smiled shakily. 'You could put it like that. It wasn't a hard promise to keep. Until I met you. But I couldn't tell you about it because it involved my parents as well as Nico. But my father likes you. It was he who urged me to tell you the truth.'

'I'm grateful to him,' said James fervently. 'And I

agree with him totally. It's time Nico knew.' His eyes narrowed. 'Hell, it's suddenly struck me—you were only a baby yourself. How on earth did it happen?'

'It wasn't rape,' she assured him quickly.

'Thank God for that!' James shifted her in his arms so he could see her face clearly. 'Can you tell me about it?' he asked gently.

'Yes. Not that there's much to tell. There was an exchange of students in Pennington when I was nearly fifteen. Some pupils from the comprehensive were playing host to students from France and Italy on an exchange arrangement during the Christmas holidays.'

'So your family had someone to stay?'

'No. I went to the convent, remember.' Eleri smiled wryly. 'But one of the sixth-formers from the other school took his homesick Italian houseguest into the trattoria for a meal one day and introduced him to my father, who invited them both to our house. It became a regular occurrence. Simon and Fabio spent hours at our place, ate Sunday lunch with us, played games with ten-year-old Claudia and took me to the cinema and so on. I had the time of my life. My schoolmates at the convent were green with envy.'

'So that's why Nico looks so Italian,' said James thoughtfully. 'So what happened to Fabio?'

'Nothing. Fabio was a respectful Italian boy. Simon was the culprit—tall, dark, with bright blue eyes, the star of the football team, owner of a motorcycle, and the object of general teenage female lust at his school.'

James shook his head, taken aback. 'Go on.'

'At almost fifteen I was the size—and shape—I am now, but with much longer hair,' said Eleri without emotion. 'One day Fabio was laid up with an upset stomach, so when I went to meet them only Simon was waiting for me. I didn't mind in the least. I was totally dazzled by him. It was a sunny, mild day for late December, but there wasn't a soul about in the woods where we went for a walk. I had been fantasising for some time about having Simon kiss me, so when he did I suppose I misled him with my girlish enthusiasm. In no time we were lying on his leather jacket on the grass and I found to my horror that I was no match for a big, randy seventeen-year-old who lost control completely and subjected me to a fumbling, painful messy experience that gave no pleasure to me—nor much to him, probably. He told me it would be better next time.' She laughed shortly. 'I screamed at him like a virago, told him there wouldn't be a next time, that I never wanted to see him again.'

'And did you?'

'No. I made myself scarce when he brought Fabio round to say goodbye. And Simon never achieved his Easter exchange holiday with Fabio's family. He came off his prized motorcycle and died instantly, a few days short of his eighteenth birthday.'

'Good God!'

'Quite so.' Eleri looked up at his intent face in

appeal. 'Now at this point you need to take into account my sheltered upbringing and convent education. I was quite sure it was Simon's punishment, and waited for God to strike me too. It didn't dawn on me for several months what form my personal punishment was taking. I thought I was stricken with some fatal disease because I felt so sick and ill at the time. Then my mother questioned me on certain matters I had always kept fiercely private and realised I was three months pregnant.'

'Poor baby,' said James huskily, and kissed her drooping mouth. 'So what happened next?'

'At this juncture,' said Eleri bleakly, 'you must bear my particular circumstances in mind, I was barely fifteen. Under-age in more ways than one. With no possibility of marriage there were three options open to me: abortion, adoption, or life as a single parent. The first two were unthinkable. So my mother and my father—who blamed himself bitterly because he was responsible for bringing Simon and me together—formed a plan.'

The school was told that Eleri was suffering from glandular fever. Officially to prevent Claudia from catching it, Eleri went off to Wales to her grandmother, who hired an isolated cottage on the Gower peninsula for the summer and gradually restored her granddaughter to sanity there. In the meantime Catrin, who had been loud with her complaints about weight gain, announced she was pregnant.

Then one hot, late August afternoon Mario drove

Catrin down to the Gower in haste, and arrived just in time to greet Niccolo Conti, who arrived a month early. After a few days Eleri pronounced herself fit, tore herself away from her beloved baby, and insisted on returning to Pennington while Catrin, who was believed to have given birth suddenly while on holiday, remained behind with her mother and Nico.

'And when the autumn term started I went back to school,' she went on. 'But thanks to my parents I wasn't separated from my baby. I owe them a great deal.'

'That was a hell of an experience for a schoolgirl,' said James with feeling. 'No wonder you keep men at arm's length.'

'Except you.'

'Except me,' he agreed, then frowned. 'Why the look?'

Eleri looked away. 'Tell me the truth. Does it make a difference, James?'

He made no pretence of misunderstanding. 'To how I feel about you? Don't talk nonsense, woman. I love you. Nothing can change that. But I agree with your parents. It's time to tell Nico. He's fifteen, just as you were when he was born, so he's exactly the right age to appreciate what you went through. If your parents think you should tell him, then do it, Eleri. I'd gladly offer myself in support, but that wouldn't be right. This is between Nico and his mother.'

'I know you're right. I'll fetch him home from hospital and make my confession.'

'Good girl. Then come round here tomorrow night and tell me what happened.'

Eleri clapped a hand to her mouth.

James frowned. 'What's up.'

'I forgot. I was supposed to ask you round for a meal. It's my birthday tomorrow.'

'I know,' said James smugly. 'Actually I'd booked a table at the Chesterton, but I'd much rather celebrate with your family. Lunch or dinner?'

'I'm not sure. I'll ring you when I get home.' She looked up with a shaky smile as the doorbell rang. 'I hope all this melodrama hasn't put you off your food—that's Luigi with our supper.'

When James presented himself at the Conti household promptly at noon the following day, he was greeted by Nico, who sported a spectacular black eye somewhat at odds with his crisp white shirt and black jeans.

'Hi, James. Are those flowers for me?'

'No fear. How are you? Still seeing stars?'

'No. Eleri's the starry-eyed one round here.' Nico ushered his guest along to the sitting room. 'Here he is, birthday girl.'

Eleri smiled at James with such radiance he put the sheaf of red roses down on the table and took her in his arms, ignoring the wolf-whistles from Nico.

'Happy birthday, darling.'

'Thirty roses, El,' said Nico, impressed.

Eleri laughed, pulling a face. 'Thank you, James—for the beautiful roses, if not the fateful number.'

'Perhaps you'd prefer these then,' said James, handing her a gift-wrapped box.

She shot a glance at him, then egged on by Nico, unwrapped her present to reveal a pair of ruby pendant earrings. 'Oh, James, how extravagant—they're exquisite.' She gave him a brilliant, sparkling smile. 'I'll buy a new red dress to do them justice.' She darted to the large gilt mirror in the hall to thread the earrings through her lobes, then ran back to him and threw her arms round his neck and kissed him. 'You're spoiling me.'

'Where are your parents?'

'Over at the trattoria,' said Nico, and glanced at his watch. 'Ouch, I'm supposed to be there too. We're lunching in the function room in honour of the birthday girl and my help is required.' He pulled a face. 'Brace yourself, James. Family parties demand stamina!'

When he'd gone James took Eleri by the elbows and looked down into her face. 'Don't keep me in suspense. Did you tell him?'

'Yes.' She shook her head in wonder. 'He already knew.'

James whistled. 'How?'

'Nico came home early one night last week, due to a cancelled football practice, and my parents came back from the trattoria thinking he was out. He was just about to run down and announce himself when he heard my mother saying it was high time Nico knew the truth.'

'So he eavesdropped.'

Eleri nodded. 'He stole back to bed afterwards and pretended to be asleep when my mother went to check on him.'

'So when he woke up in hospital and said "Mamma", he wasn't confusing you with your mother,' James said slowly.

'No. He said he'd always felt closer to me than Claudia. Which isn't surprising. From the moment my mother brought him home I shared the responsibility of looking after him— nappies, feeding, sterilising, the lot. But Claudia adores him too. Between us we taught him to walk and talk, and I used to read to him by the hour.'

'So it came as no great surprise to him, then?'

'Not really. But he'd been worried sick about the identity of his father. Nico knows all too much about rape and assault from television. His relief was enormous when I told him that his father was a perfectly nice boy I had a crush on. Especially when I told him Simon was a bit of a star on the football field.' She pushed her hair behind her ears, her eyes suspiciously shiny. 'It won't alter anything. Nico loves my parents as much as they love him. Thank God, he doesn't seem bothered by it all—he even joked about having three parents instead of two.'

'Are there any grandparents he should know about?'

Eleri shook her head. 'Simon was brought up by his grandmother. I went to see her after Nico was born, but she was very ill. She couldn't understand who I was, so I didn't try to tell her. She died not long afterwards. Nico's all mine,' she added fiercely.

'Could you love any children of ours as much?' asked James bluntly.

Eleri stood very still. 'Oh, yes. Of course I could.' She smiled at him happily. 'How many would you like?'

The birthday lunch to celebrate Eleri Conti's thirtieth birthday was a memorable occasion, everyone gathered there intent on having a wonderful time and doing full justice to the lavish display of Welsh and Italian cuisine. When James arrived with Eleri, he managed a few minutes in private with her parents before she took him on a round of introductions—which included her pretty, heavily pregnant sister Claudia, who had insisted on coming despite her anxious young husband's fears.

'Miss a birthday party?' she declared, beaming at James. 'Not to mention meeting you! I insisted Paul bring me.'

'No problem eating for two here, Claudia,' said Nico, grinning. 'We could feed half of Pennington with this lot.'

The Contis had invited neighbours and friends, including a very shy Lucy, plus Mrs Bronwen Hughes, who had arrived by train from Cardiff the night before.

'This is James Kincaid, Grandma,' said Eleri.

'How do you do?' said Mrs Hughes, eyeing him searchingly.

'I'm very glad to know you,' responded James, and returned the look very steadily. 'Eleri's told me a lot about you.'

The fierce black eyes softened. 'Has she indeed? All good, I hope?'

'Astonishingly so,' he assured her, and gave her the smile her granddaughter found so irresistible.

The party went with a swing from the first, not least because Catrin and Mario Conti were so very obviously enjoying themselves as much as their guests. It was late in the afternoon when Mario got to his feet and raised his glass, asking his guests to join him in a birthday toast to his daughter.

There was a chorus of greetings round the table as the guests drank to Eleri, then Mario rapped on the table again for silence. 'And now another toast, again to my daughter Eleri, but this time also to her future husband, Mr James Kincaid.'

There were exclamations of surprise and pleasure, and calls for Eleri to make a speech. She shook her head, smiling, and James rose to his feet and thanked his host for a wonderful meal, expressing much pleasure at meeting family and friends. 'And last, but not least, I thank you all for your good wishes to Eleri and myself.' He took a familiar box from his pocket and opened it, then slid the ruby ring on Eleri's finger to a deafening cheer from the gathered company.

Suddenly there was a gasp from Claudia. Her husband Paul bent over her in panic and Catrin and Eleri almost cannoned into each other in their haste to get to her.

'Is it the baby?' demanded her mother.

'Yes.' Claudia managed a lopsided smile. 'Sorry to leave so soon, but I think someone else wants to join the party.'

James suggested Nico bring his Lucy along to Chester Gardens to wait for news, leaving the Contis at home with Mrs Hughes.

'I'll ring you as soon as Paul lets us know,' said Catrin, and reached up to give James a kiss. 'Welcome to the family, James. I hope it wasn't too much for you today.'

'It was a great party, Mrs Conti,' he assured her. 'My grateful thanks. When my parents come over from France I'll get my sister and her family up from London and we'll have another one. On me, this time.'

'We shall be delighted,' said Mario, and looked at Nico with a commanding eye. 'Take Lucy home in good time, my son.'

'Will do,' said Nico cheerfully.

'I'm afraid we'll all have to walk.' said James ruefully. 'The wine you served was so superb I indulged too much, Mr Conti. I daren't drive.'

'Mario, please,' said her father, to Eleri's surprise.

'You made a hit with Pa,' remarked Nico as they set out for Chester Gardens. 'Probably grateful—thought he'd never get Eleri off his hands.'

'Nico!' said Lucy, scandalised, but Eleri laughed and gave him a not too gentle shove.

'Any more of that and we'll let you go hungry when we get home.'

James gave her an appalled look. 'Are we obliged to feed these two as well as keep them out of mischief?'

'Are you sure it isn't the other way round?' said Nico slyly. 'Luce and I are coming along to play gooseberry.'

Despite the banter over a cold supper, as the evening wore on Eleri couldn't help feeling anxious. Her own experience of childbirth had been protracted and agonising, and she hoped fervently that Claudia's would be easier. She looked up from the Monopoly board at one stage to intercept a look which told her Nico was reading her thoughts. He smiled at her affectionately, then gave a furious exclamation as he landed on Lucy's Mayfair property.

'You're going to clean me out, Luce. If I'd known you were such a whiz at this I'd have voted for Trivial Pursuit.'

'She's probably a whiz at that too,' said James dryly.

Lucy, who was a lot more at home in their company by this time, nodded matter-of-factly. 'We play at lot of board games at home.' She gave Nico a sweet little smile. 'I'm good at Maths too.'

When the phone rang just after eight James grabbed it and tossed it to Eleri, who listened to her mother's jubilant voice with relief, then rang off and turned to the others, beaming. 'Caterina Paula arrived a few minutes ago. Mother and baby doing well, father shattered! Ma sent you a message, by the way, Nico.'

'I know! Take Lucy home in good time, come straight home afterwards, and no hanging about because it's school tomorrow, bang on the head or not,' he chanted.

James laughed at the wicked reproduction of Catrin's accent. 'She can't have said all that, Eleri?'

'No. But the general drift was there, so let's pack this lot up and speed these two on their way.'

While Lucy was downstairs in the bathroom Nico looked from Eleri to James rather awkwardly. 'I haven't congratulated you both. But I'm glad. About a lot of things.' He gave Eleri a hug, and a hurried, clumsy kiss. 'It hasn't sunk in properly yet—you look too young to be my mother.' He grinned at James. 'And I promise not to call you Dad, either.'

'That's a relief,' said James promptly. 'Otherwise I'd ask for my ring back.'

'Ask as much as you like,' said Eleri, waving her left hand about admiringly to hide her emotion. 'The only way you get this is with finger attached.' She looked up as the doorbell rang. 'Right, then—come on, Lucy. James is treating you to a taxi.'

Nico flushed as James handed him a banknote to pay for it. 'This is too much.'

'Keep the change,' said James, and grinned. 'Don't worry, this is a one-off. Any other night you walk.'

'That was very nice of you,' said Eleri as they waved the younger pair off.

'I am nice,' he said, smiling and closed the door. 'So come inside, my pretty one, and thank me in the way I like best.'

'I like it too,' she admitted, fluttering her eyelashes.

James let his eyes wander over her in leisurely scrutiny, from the black velvet trousers to the tawny silk shirt which clashed so vividly with the ruby earrings. 'You look like twenty tonight, not thirty.'

'It's the relief of Nico's reaction, plus Caterina's safe arrival, *and* the fact that I've just got engaged to the most wonderful man in the world,' she said extravagantly.

'Oh, I wouldn't say that,' said James modestly. 'There must be one or two others around.'

Eleri shook her head, suddenly serious. 'Not for me.'

James looked at her for a moment, then glanced at his watch. 'It's nearly nine, Cinderella. I assume you want to be home by midnight.'

'Afraid so.'

'Would it shock you to know that I'm desperate to make love to my future wife?'

'Not in the least.'

'Then what would you say if I suggest taking some champagne downstairs for a private, passionate celebration of our own?'

'I thought you'd never ask!'

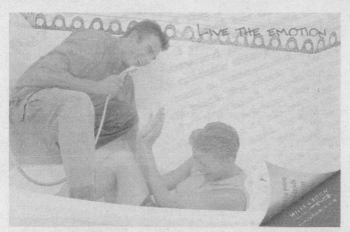

Modern Romance™
...international affairs
– seduction and
passion guaranteed

Medical Romance™
...pulse-raising
romance – heart-
racing medical drama

Tender Romance™
...sparkling, emotional,
feel-good romance

Sensual Romance™
...teasing, tempting,
provocatively playful

Historical Romance™
...rich, vivid and
passionate

Blaze Romance™
...scorching hot
sexy reads

27 new titles every month.

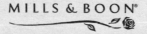

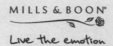

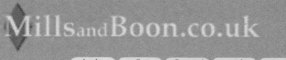